"I despise you."

He uncoiled his body like a lazy cat and came toward her.

"Liking me isn't a prerequisite for the night we're about to spend together."

"We aren't," she said quickly, even though she knew he was baiting her, that he was really just referring to the time she'd be with him at the party. "There's no way I'd spend the night with—"

He bent and brushed his mouth over hers. That was all he did; the kiss was little more than a whisper of flesh to flesh, but the intake of her breath more than proved she was lying.

She knew it. He knew it. And she hated him for it.

"The Sheik," she said, her eyes cool.

"I beg your pardon?"

"The Sheik, starring Rudolph Valentino. It's an old movie. Be sure to rent the video sometime."

Nick laughed. He held out his arm. She tossed her head. "Take it," he said softly, "unless you'd rather I lift you into my arms and carry you."

Dear Reader,

Your response to THE BARONS has been over-whelming! Thank you for welcoming this family into your hearts.

You've told me how very real Gage, Travis, Slade and Caitlin have become to you. They're just as real to me. My characters always seem to become flesh and blood as I write about them, but I have to admit that the Barons, and the Texas ranch that's home to Jonas and his wife, Marta, have taken on a special meaning. So many people pass through the Barons' lives.... I can almost hear them asking me to tell you their stories.

Welcome, then, to *Mistress of the Sheikh*. Amanda Benning is one of Jonas Baron's stepdaughters. She's happy with her independence—until gor-geous, sexy Sheikh Nicholas al Rashid thinks she's his birthday gift. Sparks fly when a man wor-shiped as the Lion of the Desert comes up against a beautiful, hot-tempered woman who thinks lions are just big pussycats in disguise.

And if you haven't read any of the other BARONS books, don't worry. You can enjoy *Mistress of the Sheikh* on its own.

With love and best wishes,

Sandra Marton

Sandra Marton loves to hear from her readers. Write to her (SASE) at P.O. Box 295, Storrs, Connecticut 06268, U.S.A.

Sandra Marton

MISTRESS OF THE SHEIKH

THE BARONS

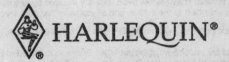

HARLEQUIN®

TORONTO • NEW YORK • LONDON
AMSTERDAM • PARIS • SYDNEY • HAMBURG
STOCKHOLM • ATHENS • TOKYO • MILAN • MADRID
PRAGUE • WARSAW • BUDAPEST • AUCKLAND

ISBN 0-373-12136-9

MISTRESS OF THE SHEIKH

First North American Publication 2000.

Copyright © 2000 by Sandra Myles.

Visit us at www.eHarlequin.com

Printed in U.S.A.

CHAPTER ONE

SHEIKH Nicholas al Rashid, Lion of the Desert, Lord of the Realm and Sublime Heir to the Imperial Throne of Quidar, stepped out of his tent and onto the burning sands, holding a woman in his arms.

The sheikh was dressed in a gold-trimmed white burnoose; his silver-gray eyes stared straight ahead, blazing with savage passion. The woman, her arms looped around his neck, gazed up at him, her face alight with an unspoken plea.

What's the matter, Nick? she'd been saying.

There's a camera pointed straight at us, Nick had answered. *That's what's the matter.*

But nobody seeing this cover on *Gossip* magazine would believe anything so simple, Nick thought grimly.

His eyes dropped to the banner beneath the picture. If words could damn a man, these surely did.

Sheikh Nicholas al Rashid, the caption said, in letters that looked ten feet tall, *carrying off his latest conquest, the beautiful Deanna Burgess. Oh, to be abducted by this gorgeous, magnificent desert savage...*

"Son of a bitch," Nick muttered.

The little man standing on the opposite side of the sparely furnished, elegant room nodded. "Yes, my lord."

"No-good, lying, cheating, sneaky bastards!"

"Absolutely," the little man said, nodding again.

Nick looked up, his eyes narrowed.

"Calling me a 'desert savage,' as if I were some kind of beast. Is that what they think I am? An uncultured, vicious animal?"

"No, sire." The little man clasped his hands together. "Surely not."

"No one calls me that and gets away with it."

But someone had, once. Nick frowned. A woman or, more accurately, a girl. The memory surfaced, wavering like a mirage from the hot sand.

Nothing but a savage, she'd said....

The image faded, and Nick frowned. "That photo was taken at the festival. It was Id al Baranda, Quidar's national holiday, for God's sake!" He stepped out from behind his massive beechwood desk and paced to the wall of windows that gave way onto one of New York City's paved canyons. "That's why I was wearing a robe, because it is the custom."

Abdul bobbed his head in agreement.

"And the tent," Nick said through his teeth. "The damned tent belonged to the caterer."

"I know, my lord."

"It was where the food was set up, dammit!"

"Yes, sire."

Nick stalked back to his desk and snatched up the magazine. "Look at this. Just look at it!"

Abdul took a cautious step forward, rose up on the balls of his feet and peered at the photo. "Lord Rashid?"

"They've taken the ocean out of the picture. It looks as if the tent was pitched in the middle of the desert!"

"Yes, my lord. I see."

Nick dragged his hand through his hair. "Miss Burgess cut her foot." His voice tightened. "That was why I was carrying her."

"Lord Rashid." Abdul licked his lips. "There is no need to explain."

"I was carrying her *into* the tent, not out. So I could treat the—" Nick stopped in midsentence and drew a ragged breath deep into his lungs. "I will not let this anger me."

"I am so glad, my lord."

"I will not!"

"Excellent, sire."

"There's no point to it." Nick put the magazine on his desk, tucked his hands into the pockets of his trousers and threw his secretary a chilling smile. "Isn't that right, Abdul?"

The little man nodded. "Absolutely."

"If these idiots wish to poke their noses into my life, so be it."

"Yes, my lord."

"If people wish to read such drivel, let them."

Abdul nodded. "Exactly."

"After all, what does it matter to me if I am called an uncultured savage?" Nick's smile tightened until his face resembled a mask. "Never mind my law degree or my expertise in finance."

"Lord Rashid," Abdul said carefully, "sire—"

"Never mind that I represent an ancient and honorable and highly cultured people."

"Excellency, please. You're getting yourself upset. And, as you just said, there is no point in—"

"The fool who wrote this should be drawn and quartered."

Abdul nodded, his head bobbing up and down like a balloon on a string. "Yes, my lord."

"Better still, staked out, naked, in the heat of the desert sun, smeared with honey so as to draw the full attention of the fire ants."

Abdul bowed low as he backed toward the door. "I shall see to it at once."

"Abdul." Nick took a deep breath.

"My Lord?"

"You are to do nothing."

"Nothing? But, Excellency—"

"Trust me," the sheikh said with a faint smile. "The part of me that is American warns me that my fellow countrymen are probably squeamish about drawing and quartering."

"In that case, I shall ask for a retraction."

"You are not to call the magazine at all."

"No?"

"No. It would serve no purpose except to bring further unwanted attention to myself, and to Quidar."

Abdul inclined his head. "As you command, Lord Rashid."

Nick reached out, turned the copy of *Gossip* toward him, handling it as gingerly as he would a poisonous spider.

"Phone the florist. Have him send six dozen red roses to Miss Burgess."

"Yes, sire."

"I want the flowers delivered immediately."

"Of course."

"Along with a card. Say…" Nick frowned. "Say that she has my apologies that we made the cover of a national magazine."

"Oh, I'm sure Miss Burgess is most unhappy to find her photo on that cover," Abdul said smoothly, so smoothly that Nick looked at him. The little man flushed. "It is most unfortunate that either of you should have been placed in such a position, my lord. I am glad you are taking this so calmly."

"I am calm, aren't I?" Nick said. "Very calm. I have counted twice to ten, once in Quidaran and once in English, and—and…" His gaze fell to the cover again. "Very calm," he murmured, and then he grabbed the magazine from the desk and flung it against the wall. "Lying sons of camel traders," he roared, and kicked the thing across the room the second it slid to the floor. "Oh, what I'd like to do to the bastards who invade my life and print such lies."

"Excellency." Abdul's voice was barely a whisper. "Excellency, it is all my fault."

The sheikh gave a harsh laugh. "Did you point a camera at me, Abdul?"

"No. No, of course—"

"Did you sell the photo to the highest bidder?" Nick swung around, his eyes hot. "Did you write a caption that makes it sound as if I'm a bad reincarnation of Rudolph Valentino?"

Abdul gave a nervous laugh. "Certainly not."

"For all I know, it wasn't even a reporter. It could have been someone I think of as a friend." Nick shoved both hands through his black-as-midnight hair. "If I ever get my hands on one of the scum-sucking dung beetles who grow fat by invading the privacy of others—''

Abdul dropped to his knees on the silk carpet and knotted his hands imploringly beneath his chin. "It is my fault, nevertheless. I should not have permitted your eyes to see such an abomination. I should have hidden it from you."

"Get up," Nick said sharply.

"I should never have let you see it. Never!"

"Abdul," Nick said more gently, "stand up."

"Oh, my lord..."

Nick sighed, bent down and lifted the little man to his feet.

"You did the right thing. I needed to see this piece of filth before the party tonight. Someone is sure to spring it on me just to see my reaction."

"No one would have the courage, sire."

"Trust me, Abdul. Someone will." A smile softened Nick's hard mouth. "My sweet little sister, if no one else. We both know how she loves to tease."

Abdul smiled, too. "Ah. Yes, yes, she does."

"So, it's a good thing you showed me the cover. I'd much rather be prepared."

"That was my belief, sire. But perhaps I erred. Perhaps I should not—"

"What would you have done instead, hmm?" Nick grinned. "Bought up all the copies from all the newsstands in Manhattan?"

Abdul nodded vigorously. "Precisely. I should have purchased all the copies, burned them—"

"Abdul." Nick put his arm around the man's shoulders and walked him toward the door. "You took the proper action. And I am grateful."

"You are?"

"Just imagine the headlines if I'd had this temper tantrum in public." Nick lifted his hand and wrote an imaginary sentence in the air. "Savage Sheikh Shows Savage Side," he said dramatically.

The little man gave him a thin smile.

"Now imagine what would happen if somebody manages to get a picture of me slicing into the cake at the party tonight."

"The caterer will surely do the slicing, sire."

Nick sighed. "Yes, I'm sure he will. The point is, anything is possible. Can you just see what the sleaze sheets would do with a picture of me with a knife in my hand?"

"In the old days," Abdul said sternly, "you could have had their heads!"

The sheikh smiled. "These are not those days," he said gently. "We are in the twenty-first century, remember?"

"You still have that power, Lord Rashid."

"It is not a power I shall ever exercise, Abdul."

"So you have said, Excellency." The man paused at the door to Nick's office. "But your father can tell you that the power to spare a man his life, or take it from him, is the best way of assuring that all who deal with you will do so with honor and respect."

A quick, satisfying picture flashed through Nick's mind. He imagined all the media people, and especially all the so-called friends who'd ever made money by selling him out, crowded into the long-unused dungeon beneath the palace back home, every last one of them pleading for mercy as the royal executioner sharpened his ax.

"It's a sweet thought," he admitted after a minute. "But that is no longer our way."

"Perhaps it should be," Abdul said, and sighed. "At any rate, my lord, there will be no unwanted guests lying in wait for you this evening."

"No?"

"No. Only those with invitations will be admitted by your bodyguards. And I sent out the invitations myself."

Nick nodded. "Two hundred and fifty of my nearest and dearest friends," he said, and smiled wryly. "That's fine."

His secretary nodded. "Will that be all, Lord Rashid?"

"Yes, Abdul. Thank you."

"You are welcome, sire."

Nick watched as the old man bowed low and backed out of the room. Don't, he wanted to tell him. You're old enough to be my grandfather, but he knew what Abdul's reply would be.

"It is the custom," he would say.

And he was right.

Nick sighed, walked to his desk and sat down in the ornately carved chair behind it.

Everything was "the custom". The way he was addressed. The way Quidarans, and even many Americans, bowed in his presence. He didn't mind it so much from his countrymen; it made him uncomfortable, all that head-bobbing and curtseying, but he understood it. It was a sign of respect.

It was, he supposed, such a sign for some Americans, too.

But for others, he sensed, it was an acknowledgment that they saw him as a different species. Something exotic. An Arab, who dressed in flowing robes. A primitive creature, who lived in a tent.

An uncultured savage, who took his women when, where and how he wanted them.

He rose to his feet and walked across the room to the windows, his mouth set in a grim line, his eyes steely.

He had worn desert robes perhaps half a dozen times in his life, and then only to please his father. He'd slept in a tent more times than that, but only because he loved the sigh of the night wind and the sight of the stars against the blackness of a sky that can only be found in the vastness of the desert.

As for women... Custom permitted him to take any that pleased him to his bed. But he'd never taken a woman who hadn't wanted to be taken. Never forced one into his bed or held one captive in a harem.

A smile tilted across Nick's mouth.

Humility was a virtue, much lauded by his father's people, and he was properly modest about most things, but why lie to himself about women? For that matter, why would he need a harem?

The truth was that women had always been there. They tumbled into his bed without any effort at all on his part, even in his university days at Yale when his real identity hadn't been known to what seemed like half the civilized world.

They'd even been there in the years before that.

Nick's smile grew.

He thought back to that summer he'd spent in L.A. with his late mother. She was an actress; it had seemed as if half the women who lived in Beverly Hills were actresses, starting with the stunning brunette next door, who'd at first taken him for the pool boy—and taken him, too, for rides far wilder than any he'd ever experienced on the backs of his father's pure-bred Arabians.

There'd always been women.

Nick's smile dimmed.

It was true, though, that some of the ones who were drawn to him now were interested more in what they might gain from being seen with him than anything else.

He knew that there were women who wanted to bask in the spotlight so mercilessly trained on him, that there were others who thought a night in his arms might lead to a lifetime at his side. There were even women who hoped to enter his private world so they could sell their stories to the scandal sheets.

His eyes went flat and cold.

Only a foolish man would involve himself with such women, and he was not a—

The phone rang. Nick snatched it from the desk.

"Yes?"

"If you're going to be here in time to shower and shave and change into a tux," his half sister's voice said with teasing petulance, "you'd better get a move on, Your Gorgeousness."

Nick smiled and hitched a hip onto the edge of the desk.

"Watch what you say to me, little sister. Otherwise, I'll have your head on the chopping block. Abdul says it's an ideal punishment for those who don't show me the proper respect."

"The only thing that's going to be cut tonight is my birthday cake. It's not every day a girl turns twenty-five."

"You forget. It's my birthday, too."

"Oh, I know, I know. Isn't it lovely, sharing a father and a birthday? But you're not as excited as I am."

Nick laughed. "That's because I'm over the hill. After all, I'm thirty-four."

"Seriously, Nick, you will be here on time, won't you?"

"Absolutely."

"Not early, though." Dawn laughed softly. "Otherwise, you'll expect me to change what I'm wearing."

Nick's brows lifted. "Will I?"

"Uh-huh."

"Meaning what you have on is too short, too low, too tight—"

"This is the twenty-first century, Your Handsomeness."

"Not when you're on Quidaran turf, it isn't. And stop calling me stuff like that."

"A," Dawn said, ticking her answers off on her fingers, "this isn't Quidaran turf. It's a penthouse on Fifth Avenue."

"It's Quidaran turf," Nick said. Dawn smiled; she could hear the laughter in his voice. "The moment I step on it anyway. What's B?"

"B, if *Gossip* can call you 'Your Handsomeness', so can I." She giggled. "Have you seen the article yet?"

"I've seen the cover," Nick said tersely. "That was enough."

"Well, the article says that you and Deanna—"

"Never mind that. You just make sure you're decently dressed."

"I *am* decently dressed, for New York."

Nick sighed. "Behave yourself, or I'll have you sent home."

"Me? Behave myself?" Dawn snorted and switched the portable phone to her other ear as she strolled through her brother's massive living room and out the glass doors to the terrace. "I'm not the one dating Miss Hunter."

"Hunter? But Deanna's name is—"

"Hunter of a titled husband. Hunter of the spotlight. Hunter of wealth and glamour—"

"She's not like that," Nick said quickly.

"Why isn't she?"

"Dawn. I am not going to discuss this with you."

"You don't have to. I know the reason. You have this silly idea that because Deanna has her own money and an old family name, she's—what's the right word—trustworthy."

Nick sighed. "Sweetheart," he said gently, "I appreciate your concern. But—"

"But you want me to mind my own business."

"Something like that, yes."

His sister rolled her eyes at the blond woman who stood with her back against the terrace wall. "Men can be clueless," she hissed.

Amanda Benning did her best to smile. "Have you told him yet?"

"No. No, not—"

"Dawn?" Nick's voice came through the phone. "Who are you talking to?"

Dawn made a face at Amanda. "One of the caterer's assistants," she said briskly. "She wanted to know where to put the cold hors d'oeuvres. And speaking of knowing, aren't you curious about what I got you for your birthday?"

"Sure. But if you told me, it wouldn't be a surprise. And birthday presents are supposed to be surprises."

"Ah. Well, I already know what my gift is."

"You do?"

"Uh-huh." Dawn grinned. "That shiny new Jaguar in the garage downstairs."

Nick groaned. "There's no keeping anything from you."

"Nope, there isn't. Now, you want to take a stab at what I'm giving you?"

"Well, there was that time you gave me a doll," Nick said dryly, "the one you wanted for yourself."

"I was seven!" Dawn grinned at Amanda. "Definitely clueless," she whispered.

"What?"

"I said, you're clueless, Nicky. About how to decorate this mansion of yours."

"It's not a mansion. It's an apartment. And I told you, I don't have time for such things. That's why I bought the place furnished."

"Furnished?" Dawn made a face at Amanda, who smiled. "How somebody could take a ten-million-dollar penthouse and make it look like a high-priced bordello is beyond me."

"If you have any idea what a bordello looks like, high-priced or low, I'll definitely send you home," Nick said, trying to sound affronted but not succeeding.

"You don't, either, dearest brother, or you'd never have the time or energy to bed all the females the tabloids link you with."

"Dawn—"

"I know, I know. You're not going to discuss such things with me." Dawn plucked a bit of lint from her skirt. "You know, Nicky, I'm not the baby you think I am."

"Maybe not. But it won't hurt if you let me go on living with an illusion."

His sister laughed. "When you see what I've bought you, that illusion will be shattered forever."

"We'll see about that." Nick's voice hummed with amusement.

Dawn grinned, covered the mouthpiece of the phone and looked at Amanda. "My brother doesn't believe you're going to shatter his illusions."

Amanda thumbed a strand of pale golden hair behind her ear. "Well, I'll just have to prove him wrong," she said, and told herself it was just plain ridiculous for an intelligent, well-educated, twenty-five-year-old woman to stand there with her knees knocking together at the prospect of being the birthday gift for a sheikh.

CHAPTER TWO

AMANDA swallowed nervously as Dawn put down the phone.

"Well," Dawn said, "that's that." She smiled. "I've laid the groundwork."

"Uh-huh." Amanda smiled, too, although her lips felt as if they were sticking to her teeth. "For disaster."

"Don't be silly. Oh, Nicky will probably balk when he realizes I've asked you to redo the penthouse. He'll growl a little, threaten murder and mayhem..." Dawn's brows lifted when she saw the expression on Amanda's face. "I'm joking!"

"Yeah, well, I'm not so sure about that." Amanda clasped her arms and shivered despite the heat of the midsummer afternoon. "I've gone toe-to-toe with your brother before, remember?"

Dawn made a face. "That was completely different. You were, what, nineteen?"

"Eighteen."

"Well."

"Well, what?"

"Well, that's my point," Dawn said impatiently. "You *didn't* go toe-to-toe with him. He had the advantage from the start. You were just a kid."

"I was your college roommate." Amanda caught her bottom lip between her teeth. "Otherwise known as The American Female With No Morals."

Dawn grinned. "Did he really call you that?"

"It may sound funny now, but if you'd been there—"

"I know how you must have felt," Dawn said, her smile fading. "After he hauled me out of the Dean's office, I thought he was going to have me shipped home and locked in the women's quarters for the rest of my life.''

"If your brother remembers me from that night—"

"If he does, I'll tell him he's wrong. Oh, stop worrying. He *won't* remember. It was the middle of the night. You didn't have a drop of makeup on, your hair was long then and probably hanging in your face. Look, if it all goes bad and Nicky gets angry at anybody for this, it'll be me.''

"I know. But still…''

Still, Amanda thought uneasily, she'd never forgotten her first, her only, meeting with Nicholas al Rashid.

Dawn had talked about him. And Amanda had read about him. The tabloids loved the sheikh: his incredible looks, his money, his power…his women.

Back then, Amanda didn't usually read that kind of thing. Her literary aspirations were just that. Literary. She'd been an English major, writing and reading poetry nobody but other English majors understood, although she'd been starting to think about changing her major to architectural design.

Whichever, the tabloids were too smarmy to catch her interest. And yet she found herself reaching for those awful newspapers at the supermarket checkout whenever she saw a photo of Dawn's brother on the front page.

Well, why wouldn't she? The man was obviously full of himself. It was like driving past an automobile accident; you didn't want to look but you just couldn't keep from doing it.

Dawn thought he was wonderful. "Nicky's a sweetheart,'' she always said. "I can't wait until you meet him.''

And, without warning, Amanda did.

It was the week before finals of their freshman year. Dawn was going to a frat party. She'd tried to convince Amanda to go, too, but Amanda had an exam in Renaissance design the next morning so she begged off, stayed in the dorm room they shared while Dawn partied.

Unfortunately, Dawn had one beer too many. She ended up sneaking into the bell tower at two in the morning along with half a dozen of the frat brothers, and they'd all decided it would be cool to play the carillon.

The campus police didn't agree. They brought Dawn and the boys down, hustled them into the security office and phoned their respective families.

Amanda was blissfully unaware of any of it. She'd crawled into bed, pulled the blanket over her head and fallen into exhausted sleep just past midnight.

A few hours later, she awoke to the pounding of a fist on the door of her dorm room. She sprang up in bed, heart pounding as hard as the fist, switched on the bedside lamp and pushed the hair out of her eyes.

"Who's there?"

"Open this door," a male voice demanded.

Visions conjured up from every horror movie she'd ever seen raced through her head. Her eyes flashed to the door, and her heartbeat went from fast to supersonic. She hadn't locked it, not with Dawn out—

"Open the door!"

Amanda scrambled from the bed, prayed her quaking knees would hold up long enough for her to fly across the room and throw the bolt—

The door burst open.

A thin, high shriek burst from her throat. A man dressed in jeans and a white T-shirt stood in the doorway, filling the space with his size, his rage, his very presence.

"I am Nicholas al Rashid," he roared. "Where is my sister?"

It took a few seconds for the name to register. This broad-shouldered man in jeans, this guy with the silver eyes and the stubbled jaw, was Dawn's brother?

She started to smile. He wasn't a mad killer after all...but he might as well have been.

The sheikh strode across the room, grabbed her by the front of her oversize D is For Design T-shirt and hauled her toward him. "I asked you a question, woman," Nicholas al Rashid said. "Where is my sister?"

To this day, it bothered Amanda that fear had nearly paralyzed her. She'd only been able to cower and stammer instead of bunching up her fist and slugging the bastard. A good right to the midsection was exactly what the tyrannical fool deserved.

But she was just eighteen, a girl who'd grown up in the sheltered world of exclusive boarding schools and summer camps. And the man standing over her was big, furious and terrifying.

So she'd swallowed a couple of times, trying to work up enough saliva so she could talk, and then she'd said that she didn't know where Dawn was.

Obviously, that wasn't the answer the sheikh wanted.

"You don't know," he said, his voice mocking hers. His hand tightened on her shirt and he hauled her even closer, close enough so she was nose to chest with him. "You don't know?"

"Dawn is—she's out."

"She's out," he repeated with that same cold sarcasm that was meant, she knew, to reduce her to something with about as much size and power as a mouse.

It got to her then. That he'd broken into her room. That he was on her turf, not his. That he was behaving as if this little piece of America was, instead, his own desert kingdom.

"Yes," she'd answered, lifting her chin as best she could, considering that his fist was wrapped in her shirt, forcing herself to meet his narrowed, silver eyes. "Yes, she's out, and even if I knew where she was, I wouldn't tell you, you—you two-bit dictator!"

She knew instantly she'd made a mistake. His face paled; a muscle knotted in his jaw and his mouth twisted in a way that made her blood run cold.

"What did you call me?" His voice was soft with the promise of malice.

"A two-bit dictator," she said again, and waited for the world to end. When, instead, a thin smile curved his mouth, she went from angry to furious. "Does that amuse you, Mr. Rashid?"

"You will address me as Lord Rashid." His smile tilted, so she could see the cruelty behind it. "And what amuses me is the realization that if we were in my country, I would have your tongue cut out for such insolence."

A drop of sweat beaded on Amanda's forehead. She had no doubt that he meant it but by then, she was beyond worrying about saying, or doing, the right thing. Never, not in all her life, had she despised anyone as she despised Nicholas al Rashid.

"This isn't your country. It's America. And I am an American citizen."

"And you are a typical American female. You have no morals."

"Oh, and you'd certainly know all about American females and morals, wouldn't you?"

His eyes narrowed. "I take it that's supposed to have some deep meaning."

"Just let go of me," Amanda said, grunting as she twisted against the hand still clutching her shirt. "Dammit, let go!"

He did. His fist opened, so quickly and unexpectedly that she stumbled backward. She stood staring at the man who'd invaded her room, her breasts heaving under the thin cotton shirt.

For the first time, he looked at her. Really looked at her. She could almost feel the touch of those silver eyes as they swept her from head to toe. He took in her sleep-tousled hair, her cotton shirt, the long length of her naked legs...

Amanda felt her face, then her body, start to burn under that arrogant scrutiny. She wanted to cover herself, put her arms over her breasts, but she sensed that to do so would give him even more of an advantage than he already had.

"Get out of my room," she said, her voice trembling.

Instead, his eyes moved over her again, this time with almost agonizing slowness. "Just look at you," he said very softly.

The words were coated with derision—derision, and something else. Amanda could hear it in his voice. She could read it in the way his eyes darkened. There was more to the message than the disparagement of American women and their morality. Despite her lack of experience, she knew that what he'd left unspoken was a statement of want and desire, raw and primitive and male.

It was three in the morning. She was alone in her room with a man twice her size, a man who wore his anger like a second skin...

A man more beautiful, and overwhelmingly masculine, than any she'd ever imagined or known in her entire life.

To her horror, she'd felt her body begin to quicken. A slow heat coiled low in her belly; her breasts lifted and her nipples began to harden so that she almost gasped at the feel of them thrusting against the thin cotton of her T-shirt.

He saw it, too.

His eyes went to her breasts, lingered, then lifted to her face. Amanda felt her heart leap into her throat as he took a step forward.

"Sire."

He moved toward her, his eyes never leaving hers. The heat in her belly swept into her blood.

"Sire!"

Amanda blinked. A little man in a shiny black suit had come into the room. He scuttled toward the sheikh, laid his hand on the sheikh's muscled forearm.

"My lord, I have located your sister."

The sheikh turned to the man. "Where is she?"

The little man looked at his hand, lying against the sheikh's tanned skin, and snatched it back. "Forgive me, sire. I did not mean to touch—"

"I asked you a question."

Abdul dropped to his knees and lowered his head until his brow almost touched the floor. "She awaits your will, Lord Rashid, in the office of the Dean of Students."

That had done it. The sight of the old man, kneeling in

obeisance to a surly tyrant, the thought of Dawn, awaiting the bully's will...

Amanda's vision cleared.

"Get out," she'd said fiercely, "before I have you thrown out. You're nothing but a—a savage. And I pity Dawn, or any woman, who has anything to do with you."

The sheikh's mouth had twisted, the hard, handsome face taking on the look of a predator about to claim its prey.

"Sire," the little man had whispered, and without another word, Nicholas al Rashid had spun on his heel and walked out of the room.

Amanda had never seen him again.

He'd taken Dawn out of school, enrolled her in a small women's college. But the two of them had remained friends through Amanda's change of careers, through her marriage and divorce.

Over the years, her encounter with the sheikh had faded from her memory.

Almost.

There were still times she awoke in the night with the feel of his eyes on her, the scent of him in her nostrils—

"Mandy," Dawn said, "your face is like an open book."

Amanda jerked her head up. Dawn grinned.

"You're still mortified, thinking about how Nicky stormed into our room all those years ago, when he was trying to find me."

Amanda cleared her throat. "Yes. Yes, I am. And you know, the more I think about this, the more convinced I am it's not going to work."

"What's not going to work? I told you, he won't remember you. And even if he does—"

"Dawn," Amanda said, reaching for the purse she'd dropped on one of the glass-topped tables on the enormous terrace, "I appreciate what you've tried to do for me. Honestly, I do. But—"

"But you don't need this job."

"Of course I need it. But—"

"You don't," Dawn said, striking a pose, "because you're going to make your name in New York by waving a magic wand. 'Hocus-pocus, I now pronounce me the decorator of the decade.'"

"Come on, Dawn," Amanda said with a little smile.

"Not that it matters, because you've found a way to pay your rent without working."

Amanda laughed.

"Well, what, then? Have you changed your mind about taking money from your mother?"

"Taking it from my stepfather, you mean." Amanda grimaced. "I don't want Jonas Baron's money. It comes with too many strings attached."

"Taking alimony from that ex of yours, then."

"Even more strings," Amanda said, and sighed. This was not a good idea. She could feel it in her bones—but only an idiot would walk away from an opportunity like this. "Okay," she said before she could talk herself out of it again, "I'll try."

"Good girl." Dawn looped her arm through Amanda's. The women walked slowly from the terrace into the living room. "Mandy, you know this makes sense. Doing the interior design for Sheikh Nicholas al Rashid's Fifth Avenue penthouse will splash your name everywhere it counts."

"Still, even if your brother agrees—"

"He has to. You're my birthday gift to him, remember?"

"Won't he care that he'll be my first client?"

"Your first New York client."

"Well, yeah. But I didn't really work when I lived in Dallas. You know how Paul felt about my having a career."

"Once I tell Nick you designed for Jonas Baron, and for Tyler and Caitlin Kincaid, he'll be sold."

Amanda came to a dead stop. "Are you nuts? Me, decorate my stepfather's house? Jonas would probably shoot anybody who tried to move a chair!"

"You did your mother's sitting room, didn't you?"

"Sure. But that was different. It was one room—"

"The room's in the Baron house, right?"

"Dawn, come on. That's hardly—"

"Well, what about the Kincaids?"

"All I did was rip out some of the froufrou, replace it with pieces Tyler had in his house in Atlanta and suggest a couple of new things. That's hardly the same as redoing a fourteen-room penthouse."

Dawn slapped her hands on her hips. "For heaven's sake, Mandy, will you let me handle this? What do you want me to say? 'Nick, this is Amanda. Remember her? The last time you met, you chewed her out for being a bad influence on me. Now she's going to spend a big chunk of your money doing something you really don't want done, and by the way, you're her very first real client.'"

Amanda couldn't help it. She laughed. "I guess it doesn't sound like much of a recommendation."

"No, it doesn't. And I thought we both just agreed you need this job."

"You're right," Amanda said glumly, "I do."

"Darned right, you do. At least redo the suite Nicky lets me use whenever I'm in town. Did you ever see such awful kitsch?" Dawn gave Amanda a quick hug when she smiled. "That's better. Just let me do the talking, okay?"

"Okay."

Dawn quickened her pace as they started up the wide staircase that led to the second floor. "We'll have to hurry. You put on that slinky red dress, fix your hair, spritz on some perfume and get ready to convince my brother he'd be crazy to turn up his regal nose at the chance to have this place done by the one, the only, the incredible Amanda Benning."

"You ever think about going into PR?"

"You can put me on the payroll after the first time your name shows up in the—oh, damn! We never finished our tour. You haven't seen Nick's suite."

"That's all right." Amanda patted the pocket of her silk trousers. "I'll transfer my camera into my evening bag."

"No, don't do that." Dawn shuddered dramatically as she

opened the door to her rooms. "If Nick sees you taking pictures, he'll figure you for a media spy and..." She grinned and sliced her hand across her throat. "How's this? You shower first, get dressed, then grab a quick look. His rooms are at the other end of the hall."

"I don't think that's a good idea," Amanda said quickly. "What if the sheikh comes in while I'm poking around?"

"He won't. Nicky promised he'd be on time, but he's always late. He hates stuff like this. You know, public appearances, being the center of attention. The longer he can delay his entrance, the better he likes it."

Amanda thought about the walking ego who'd shoved his way into her room, unasked and unannounced.

"I'll bet," she said, and softened the words with a smile. "But I'd still feel more comfortable if you were with me."

"I promise I'll join you just as soon as I turn myself into the gorgeous, desirable creature we both know I am. Okay?"

Amanda hesitated, told herself she was being an idiot, then nodded. "Okay."

"Good." Dawn kicked off her shoes. "In that case, the shower's all yours."

Twenty minutes later, Amanda paused outside the door to the sheikh's rooms.

If anybody took her pulse right now, they'd probably enter the result in the record books. She could feel it galloping like a runaway horse, but why wouldn't it?

It wasn't every day she sneaked into a man's bedroom to take pictures and make notes. Into the bedroom of a man who demanded people address him as "Lord". A man to whom other men bowed.

Instinct told her to turn tail and run. Necessity told her to stop being a coward. She was wasting time, and there really wasn't much to waste. Ten minutes, if Dawn was wrong and the sheikh showed up promptly.

She ran a nervous hand through the short, pale gold hair

that framed her face, took the tiny digital camera from her evening purse and tapped at the door.

"Sheikh Rashid?"

There was no answer. The only sounds that carried through the vastness of the penthouse were snatches of baroque music from the quartet setting up in the library far below.

Amanda straightened her shoulders, opened the door and stepped inside the room.

It was clearly a man's domain. Dawn had said her brother hadn't changed any of the furnishings in the penthouse and Amanda could believe that—everywhere but here. This one room bore a stamp that she instantly knew was the sheikh's.

She didn't know why she would think it. Asked to describe a room Nicholas al Rashid would design for himself, she'd have come up with mahogany furniture. Dark crimson walls. Velvet drapes.

These walls were pale blue silk. The furniture was satin-finished rosewood, and the tall windows had been left un-adorned to frame the view of Central Park. The carpet was Persian, she was sure, and old enough to date back to a century when that had been the name of the country in which it had been made.

A sleek portable computer sat open on a low table.

The room spoke of simplicity and elegance. It spoke, too, of a time older than memory that flowed into a time yet to come.

Amanda began taking photos. The room. The bed. The open windows and the view beyond. She worked quickly while im-ages of the sheikh flashed through her mind. She could see him in this room, tall and leanly muscled, stiff with regal ar-rogance. He belonged here.

Then she saw the oil painting on the wall. She hesitated, then walked toward it, eyes lifted to the canvas.

The room was a sham. All the sophistication, the urban-ity…a lie, all of it. This was the real man, the one she'd met that night, and never mind the jeans and T-shirt he'd worn then, and the nonsense about his half-American ancestry.

The painting was of Nicholas al Rashid dressed in desert robes of white trimmed with gold, seated on the back of a white horse that looked as wild as he did. One hand held the reins; the other lay on the pommel of the elaborate saddle.

And his eyes, those silver eyes, seemed to be staring straight at her.

Amanda took a step back.

She was wrong to have come here, wrong to have let Dawn convince her she could take this job, even if the sheikh permitted it.

Wrong, wrong, wrong—

"What in hell do you think you're doing in my bedroom?"

The tiny camera fell from Amanda's hand. She swung around, heart racing, and saw the Lion of the Desert, the Heir to the Imperial Throne of Quidar, standing in the doorway, just as he'd been doing that night in her dormitory room.

No jeans and T-shirt this time.

He wore a dark gray suit, a white-on-white shirt and a dark red tie. He was dressed the same as half the men in Manhattan—but it was easy to imagine him in his flowing robes and headdress, with the endless expanse of the desert behind him instead of the marble hall.

Maybe it had something to do with the way he stood, legs apart, hands planted on his hips, as if he owned the world. Maybe it was the look on his hard, handsome face that said he was emperor of the universe and she was nothing but an insignificant subject....

Get a grip, Amanda.

The man had caught her off guard that night, but it wouldn't happen again. She wasn't eighteen anymore, and she'd learned how to deal with hard men who thought they owned the world, men like her father, her stepfather, her ex-husband.

Whatever else they owned, they didn't own her.

"Well? Are you deaf, woman? I asked you a question."

Amanda bent down, retrieved her camera and tucked it into her beaded evening purse.

"I heard you," she said politely. "It's just that you startled me, Sheikh Rashid.'' She took a breath, then held out her hand. ''I'm Amanda Benning.''

''And?'' he said, pointedly ignoring her outstretched hand.

''Didn't your sister tell you about me?''

''No.''

No? Oh. Dawn? Dawn, where are you?

Amanda smiled politely. ''Well, she, um, she invited me here tonight.''

''And that gives you the right to sneak into my bedroom?''

''I did not sneak,'' she said, trying to hold the smile. ''I was merely…'' Merely what? Dawn was supposed to handle all this. It was her surprise.

''Yes?''

''I was, um, I was…'' She hesitated. ''I think it's better if Dawn explains it.''

A chilly smile angled across his mouth. ''I'd much rather hear your explanation, Ms. Benning.''

''Look, this is silly. I told you, your sister and I are friends. Why not simply ask her to—''

''My sister is young and impressionable. It would never occur to her that you'd use your so-called friendship for your own purposes.''

''I beg your pardon?''

The sheikh took a step forward. ''Who sent you here?''

''Who *sent* me?'' Amanda's eyes narrowed. Nearly eight years had gone by, and he was as arrogant and overbearing as ever. Well, she wasn't the naive child she'd been the last time they'd dealt with each other, and she wasn't frightened of bullies. ''No one sent me,'' she said as she started past him. ''And there's not enough money in the world to convince me to—''

His hand closed on her wrist with just enough pressure to make her gasp.

''Give me the camera.''

She looked up at him. His eyes glittered like molten silver. She felt a lump of fear lodge just behind her breastbone, but she'd sooner have choked on the fear than let him know he'd been able to put it there.

"Let go of me," she said quietly.

His grasp on her wrist tightened; he tugged her forward. Amanda stumbled on her high heels and threw out a hand to stop herself. Her palm flattened against his chest.

It was like touching a wall of steel. The cover photo from *Gossip* sprang into her head. Savage, the caption had called him, just as she had, that night.

"Or what?" His words were soft; his smile glittered. "You are in my home, Ms. Benning. To all intents and purposes, that means you stand on Quidaran soil. My word is law here."

"That's not true."

"It is true if I say it is."

Amanda stared at him in disbelief. "Mr. Rashid—"

"You will address me as Lord Rashid," he said, and she saw the sudden memory spark to life in his eyes. "We've met before."

"No," Amanda said, too quickly. "No, we haven't."

"We have. Something about you is familiar."

"I have that kind of face. You know. Familiar."

Nick frowned. She didn't. The pale hair. The eyes that weren't brown or green but something more like gold. The elegant cheekbones, the full, almost pouty lower lip...

"Let go of my wrist, Sheikh Rashid."

"When you give me your camera."

"Forget it! It's my cam— Hey. Hey, you can't..."

He could, though Nick had to admit, it wasn't easy. The woman was twisting like a wildcat, trying to break free and keep him from opening her purse at the same time, but he hung on to her with one hand while he dug out her camera with the other.

She was still complaining, her voice rising as he thumbed from image to image. What he saw made him crazy. Photos of his home. The terrace. The living room. The library. The bathrooms, for God's sake.

And his bedroom.

She had done more than invade his privacy. She had stolen

it and would sell it to the highest bidder. He had no doubt of that.

He looked up from the digital camera, his eyes cold as they assessed her.

She was a thief, but she was beautiful even in a city filled with beautiful women. She seemed so familiar...but if they'd met before, surely he'd remember. What man would forget such a face? Such fire in those eyes. Such promised sweetness in that lush mouth.

And yet, for all of that, she was a liar.

Nick looked down at the little camera in his hand.

Beautiful, and duplicitous.

She played dangerous games, this woman. Games that took her into a man's bedroom and left her vulnerable to whatever punishment he might devise.

He lifted his head slowly, and his eyes met hers.

"Who paid you to take these pictures?"

"I can't tell you."

"Well, that's progress. At least you admit you're doing this for money."

"I am. But it isn't what you—"

"You came here in search of information. A story. Photos. Whatever you could find that was salable." A muscle flexed in his jaw. "Do you know what the punishment in my country is for those who steal?"

"Steal?" Amanda gave an incredulous laugh. "I did not—"

"Theft is bad enough," he said coldly. "Don't compound it by lying."

His eyes were flat with rage. Amanda's heart thumped. Dealing with her father, her stepfather, even her ex, was nothing compared to dealing with a man who ruled a kingdom. She wasn't one of his subjects, but she had the feeling this wasn't exactly the time to point that out.

If Nick finds out, Dawn had said, *he'll be angry at me.*

But Dawn was among the missing, the sheikh was blocking

the doorway, and clearly, discretion was not the better part of valor.

"All right." Amanda stood straighter, even though her heart was still trying to fight its way out of her chest. "I'll tell you the truth."

"An excellent decision, Ms. Benning."

She licked her lips. "I'm—I'm your surprise."

Nick frowned. "I beg your pardon?"

"My services. They're your gift. What Dawn talked about, on the phone."

His gift? Nick's brows lifted. His little sister had a strange sense of humor, but how far would she go for a joke? It could be that Amanda Benning was willing to tell one gigantic whopper as a cover story.

"Indeed," he purred.

Amanda didn't like the tone in his voice.

"I'll have you know that I'm much sought after." *Oh, Amanda, what a lie.* "And expensive." Well, why not? She would be, one day.

"Yes," Nick said softly. "That, at least, must be the truth."

And then, before she could take a breath, Nick reached for the blonde with the golden eyes and the endless legs, pulled her into his arms, and crushed her mouth under his.

CHAPTER THREE

IF THERE was one thing Nick understood, it was the art of diplomacy.

He was the heir to the throne of an ancient kingdom. He represented his people, his flag, his heritage. And he never forgot that.

It was his responsibility to behave in a way that gave the least offense to anyone, even when he was saying or doing something others might not like. He understood that obligation and accepted it.

But when the spotlight was off and Nick could be himself, the truth was that he often had trouble being diplomatic. There were instances when diplomacy was about as useful as offering condolences to a corpse. Sometimes, being polite could distract from the truth and confuse things.

He wanted no confusion in Amanda Benning's mind when it came to him. She was sophisticated and beautiful, a woman who lived by her wits as well as her more obvious charms, but he was on to her game.

And he wanted to be sure she knew it.

That was the reason he'd taken her in his arms. He was very clear about the purpose, even as he gathered her close against him, bent her back over his arm and kissed her.

He'd caught her by surprise. He'd intended that. She gasped, which gave him the chance to slip his tongue between her lips. Then she began to fight him.

Good.

She'd planned everything so carefully. The tiny camera that he should never have noticed. The sexy dress. The soft scent of her perfume. The strappy black silk shoes with the high, take-me heels...

Seduction first, conveniently made simple by his foolish sister, whose penchant for silly jokes had finally gotten out of hand. And then, having bedded the Lion of the Desert, the Benning woman would sell her photographs and a breathless first-person account of what it was like to sleep with him.

Nick caught Amanda's wrist as she struggled to shove a hand between them. What a fool Dawn had been to hire a woman like this and bring her into their midst. But he'd have been a greater fool not to at least taste her.

He wouldn't take her to bed. He was too fastidious to take the leavings of other men, but he'd give her just enough of an encounter to remember. Kiss her with harsh demand. Cup her high, lush breasts with the easy certainty that spoke of royal possession.

When she responded, not out of desire but because that was her job, he'd shove her from him, let her watch him grind her camera under his heel. After that, he'd call for Abdul and direct him to hustle the lady straight out the door.

Then he'd go in search of his sister. Dawn needed to be reminded how dangerous it was to consort with scum. A few months in Quidar, under the watchful eye of their father, would work wonders.

That was Nick's plan anyway.

The kiss, the reality of it, changed everything.

Amanda had stopped struggling. That was good. She'd been paid to accept his kisses, welcome his hands as they caressed her pliant body…except, he suddenly realized, she wasn't pliant.

She was rigid with what seemed to be fear.

Fear?

She'd cried out as his mouth covered hers. A nice touch, he'd thought coldly, that little intake of breath, that high, feminine cry. Righteous indignation didn't go with the dress or the heels, certainly not with the face or the body, but he could see where she might try it, just to heighten the tension and his arousal before her ultimate surrender.

There were games men and women played, and a woman

like this would know them all. Either Amanda Benning was
an excellent actress or he'd started the game before she was
ready.

Was she the kind who wanted to direct the performance and
the pace? Or was her imagination running wild? Innocent
maiden. Savage sheikh. The story wasn't new. Nick had come
across women who hungered for it and would accept nothing
else, but he never obliged. It was a stereotype, a fantasy that
offended him deeply, and he refused to play it out.

Sex between a man and a woman involved as much giving
as taking or it brought neither of them pleasure.

But this was different.

He had neither wooed the Benning woman nor won her.
She hadn't seduced him with a smile, a glance, a touch. She
was here because his sister had decided it would be amusing
to give her to him as a gift.

In other words, none of the usual rules applied.

The woman was his. He could do as he wanted with her.
And if what she thought he wanted was some rough sex, he
could oblige. He could play along until it was time to toss her
out.

A little rough treatment, maybe even a scare, was exactly
what Amanda Benning deserved. She was a creature of no
morals, willing to offer her body for information she could
sell to the highest bidder.

Oh, yes. A little scare would do Amanda Benning just fine.

She was struggling in earnest now, not just trying to drag
her mouth from his but fighting him, shoving her fists against
his chest, doing her best to free herself from his arms.

Nick laughed against her mouth, spun her around, pressed
her back against the silk-covered wall. He caught her wrists,
entwined his fingers with hers and flattened her hands against
the wall on either side of her.

She tried to scream. He caught her bottom lip in his teeth,
moved closer, brushed his body against her.

God, she was so warm. Heat seemed to radiate from her
skin. And she was soft. Her breasts. Her belly. Her mouth.

Her hot, luscious mouth. He could taste it now, not only the fear but what lay beyond it, the sweet taste of the woman herself.

His body hardened, became steel. There was a roaring in his ears. Nick wanted to carry her to the bed, strip her of her clothes, bury himself deep inside her. Need for her sang in his blood, raced through every muscle.

The part of his brain that still functioned told him he was insane. He was kissing a woman his sister had bought as a joke, a woman with a bag filled with professional tricks. She was pretending she didn't want him, and he was, what?

He was getting turned on.

It was just that she fitted his arms so well. That her hair felt so silken against his cheek. That she smelled sweet, the way he'd assumed she would taste. The way he wanted her to taste, he thought. The hell with it. She wanted to give a performance? All right. He would comply, but he was changing the rules.

He wasn't going to take her. He was going to seduce her.

"Amanda," he said softly.

Her lashes flew up. Her eyes met his.

"Don't fight me," he whispered, and kissed her. Gently. Tenderly. His mouth moved against hers, over and over; his teeth nipped lightly at her bottom lip. And, gradually, her mouth began to soften. She made a little sound, a whimper, and her body melted against his.

Nick groaned at the stunning sweetness of her surrender. He wanted to let go of her wrists and slide his hands down her spine, stroke the satin that was her skin, cup her bottom and lift her up into the urgency of his erection. When her hands tugged at his, seeking freedom, pleasure rocketed through him. He understood what she wanted, that she sought the freedom to touch him, explore him. It was what he wanted, too. He'd forgotten everything except that he was on fire for the woman in his arms.

He touched the tip of his tongue to the seam of her lips as he let go of her wrists and took her face in his hands. His

palms cupped her cheeks; he tilted her head back so that her
golden hair feathered like silk over the tips of his fingers, so
that he could slant his mouth hungrily over hers—

—*so that her knee could catch him right where he lived and
drive every last breath of air from his lungs.*

A strangled gasp of agony burst from his lips. Nick doubled
over and clutched his groin.

"Amanda?" he croaked, and got his chin up just in time to
see her coming at him again.

"You no-good bastard!"

He was hurting. The pain was gut-deep, but he fought it,
jumped out of her path, caught her as she flew by and flung
her on the bed. She landed hard, rolled to her side, sat up and
almost got her feet on the floor, but by then he'd recovered
enough to come down on top of her.

She called him a name he'd only heard a couple of times
in his life and pummeled him with her fists.

"Get off me!"

It was like wrestling with a wildcat. She was small and
slender but she moved fast, and it didn't help that it still felt
as if his scrotum was seeking shelter halfway up his belly.

Nick took a blow on his chin, another in the corner of his
eye. He grabbed for her hands, captured them and pinned them
high over her head.

"You little bitch," he said, straddling her hips.

Amanda bucked like an unbroken mare, her hips arcing up,
then down.

"Stop it." He leaned toward her, his eyes hot with anger.
"Damn you, woman, did you hear what I said? Stop!"

She didn't. She bucked again, her body moving against his,
her breasts heaving, her golden hair disheveled against the
blue silk pillows. Her eyes were wild, the pupils huge and
black and encircled by rims of gold. She was panting through
parted lips; he could see the flash of her small white teeth, the
pink of her tongue. Her excuse of a dress was ruined; one thin
red silk strap hung off her shoulder, exposing the upper curve
of a creamy breast. The skirt had ridden up her hips. He could

see the strip of black lace that hid the feminine delta between her thighs.

And all at once, he felt fine. No more pain, just the realization that he was hard, swollen and aroused, separated from the woman beneath him by nothing but his trousers and that scrap of sexy lace.

The air in the room crackled with electricity.

He became still. She did, too. Her eyes met his, and for the first time, what he saw in them took his breath away.

"No," she whispered, but his mouth was already coming down on hers.

She held back; he could feel her tremble.

"Yes," he said softly, and kissed her again. "Amanda..."

She moaned. Her lashes fell to her cheeks and she opened her mouth to his. Her surrender was real. Her need was, too. He could feel it in the pliancy of her body, taste it in the silken heat of her kiss.

Nick let go of her hands and gathered her against him. She moaned again and dug her hands into his hair, clutching the dark curling strands with greedy fists.

Greedy. Yes, that was the way she felt. Greedy for his mouth, for his touch. For the feel of Nicholas al Rashid deep inside her.

It was crazy. She didn't know this man, and what little she did know, she didn't like. Moments ago, she'd been fighting him off....

Her breath caught as he rolled onto his side and took her with him. He stroked his hand down her spine, then up again. All the way up, so that his thumbs brushed lightly over her breasts.

"Tell me you want me," he said.

His voice was as soft as velvet, as rough as gravel. His breath whispered against her throat as he licked the flesh where her neck joined her shoulder, and she moaned.

"Tell me," he urged, and she did by seeking his mouth with hers.

Nick sat up, tore off his suit jacket and his tie. She heard

the buttons on his shirt pop as he stripped it off. Then he came
back down to her, cupped her breasts in his hands and took
her mouth.

His skin was hot against hers. She made a little sound of
need, nipped his bottom lip. "Yes," she said, "yes, oh,
yes…"

His knee was between her thighs. She lifted herself to it,
against it; his thumbs rolled across her silk-covered nipples
and she was caught up on a wave of heat, up and up and up.
She cried out his name, shut her eyes, tossed her head from
side to side.

"Look at you," Nick whispered. "Just look at you."

And as quickly as that, it was all over.

Amanda froze. Disgust, horror, anguish…a dozen different
emotions raced through her, brought back by those simple,
unforgotten words. They took her back seven years to that
dormitory room, to the terrifying intruder named Nicholas al
Rashid who'd branded her as immoral even as he'd looked at
her and wanted her.

Bile rose in her throat. "Get off me," she said.

The sheikh didn't hear her. Couldn't hear her. She looked
up at him, hating what she saw, hating herself for being the
cause. His silver eyes were blind with desire; the bones of his
face were taut with it.

Nausea roiled in her belly. "Get—off!"

She struck out blindly, fists beating against his chest and
shoulders. He blinked; his eyes opened slowly as if he were
awakening from a dream.

"You—get—the—hell—off," she said, panting, and struck
him again.

He caught her flailing hands, pinioned them. "It's too late
to play that game."

His voice was low and rough; the hands that held her were
hard and cruel. She told herself not to panic. This was Dawn's
brother. He was arrogant, imperious and all-powerful…but he
wasn't crazy.

"Taking a woman against her will isn't a game," she said, and tried to keep the fear from her voice.

"Against her will?"

His eyes moved over her and she flushed at the slow, deliberate scrutiny. She knew how she must look. Her dress torn. The hem of her skirt at her thighs. Her lips bare of everything but the imprint of his.

A thin smile started at the corner of his mouth. "When a woman all but begs a man to take her, it's hardly 'against her will'."

"I'd never beg a man for anything," she said coldly. "And if you don't let go and get off me, I'll scream. There must be a hundred people downstairs by now. Every one of them will hear me."

"You disappoint me." The bastard didn't just smile this time; he laughed. "You sneaked into my home—"

"I didn't sneak into anything. Your sister invited me."

"Did she tell you that once the party begins, no one will be permitted on this floor?"

Her heart thumped with fear. "They will, if they hear me screaming."

"My men would not permit it."

"The police don't need your permission."

"The police can't do anything to help you. This is Quidaran soil."

"It's a penthouse on Fifth Avenue," Amanda said, trying to free her hands, "not an embassy."

"We have no embassy in your country. By the time our governments finish debating the point, it will be too late."

"You're not frightening me."

It was a lie and they both knew it. She was terrified; Nick could see it in her eyes. Good. She'd deserved the lesson. She was immoral. She was a liar. A thief. She was for sale to any man who could afford her.

What did that make him, then, for still wanting her?

Nick let go of her hands, rolled off her and got to his feet. "Get out," he said softly.

She sat up, moved to the edge of the bed, her eyes wary. She shot a glance at the door and he knew she was measuring her chances of reaching it. It made him feel rotten but, dammit, she wasn't worth his pity. She wasn't worth anything except, perhaps, the price his foolish sister had paid for her.

"Go on," he said gruffly, and jerked his head toward the door. "Get out, before I change my mind."

She rose from the bed. Smoothed down her skirt with hands that shook. Bent and picked up her purse, grabbed the camera and put it inside.

She stumbled backward as Nick came around the bed toward her.

"No," she said sharply, but he ignored her, snatched the purse from her hands and opened the flap. "What are you doing?"

He looked up. He had to give her points for courage, he thought grudgingly. She'd lost one of her ridiculously high heels in their struggle. Her dress was a mess and her hair hung in her eyes.

Those unusual golden eyes.

He frowned, reached for a memory struggling to the surface of his mind....

"Give me my purse."

She lunged for the small beaded bag. He whipped it out of her reach. She went after it, lifting up on her toes and batting at it with her hands.

"Dammit, give me that!"

Nick took out the camera and tossed the purse at her feet. "It's all yours."

"I want my camera."

"I'm sure you do."

Grinding the camera to dust under his heel would have been satisfying, but the carpet was soft and he knew he might end up looking like an ass if the damned thing didn't break. Instead, he strolled into the bathroom.

"What are you...?"

Nick pressed a button on the camera, took out the tiny recording disk and dumped it into the toilet. He shut the lid, flushed, then dropped the camera on the marble floor. Now, he thought, now it would smash when he stepped on it.

It did.

Amanda Benning was scarlet with fury. "You—you bastard!"

"My parents would be upset to hear you call me that, Ms. Benning," he said politely. He walked past her, pleased that the toilet hadn't spit the disk back—it had been a definite possibility and it surely would have spoiled the drama of the moment.

A little more drama, and he'd send Amanda Benning packing.

He swung toward her and folded his arms over his chest. "Actually, addressing me in such a fashion could get you beheaded in my homeland."

Amanda planted her hands on her hips. "It could get you sued in mine."

He laughed. "You can't sue me. I'm—"

"Believe me, I know who you are, Mr. Rashid."

"Lord Rashid," Nick said quickly, and scowled.

What was he saying? He didn't care about his title. Everyone used it. It was the custom but occasionally someone forgot, and he never bothered correcting them. The only time he had was years ago. Dawn's roommate...

The girl with the golden eyes. Strange that he should have remembered her after so long a time. Stranger still that he should have done so tonight.

"...and ninety-eight cents."

He blinked, focused his eyes on Amanda Benning. She hadn't moved an inch. She was still standing in front of him, chin lifted, eyes flashing. He felt a momentary pity that she was what she was. A woman as beautiful, as fiery as this, would be a true gift, especially in a man's bed.

"Did you hear me, *Lord* Rashid?" Amanda folded her arms, tapped her foot. "You owe me $620.98. That includes the film."

One dark, arched brow lifted. It made him look even more insolent. She was boring him, she thought, and fought back a tremor of rage.

"I beg your pardon?"

"The camera." She marched past him, plucked her purse from the floor, dug inside it and pulled out a rumpled piece of paper. "The receipt. From Picture Perfect, on Madison Avenue."

She held it out. Nick looked at it but didn't touch it.

"An excellent place to buy electronic devices, or so I've been told."

"I want my money."

"What for?"

"I just told you. For the camera you destroyed."

"Ah. That."

"Yes. Yes, 'Ah, that.' You owe me six hundred and—"

Nick reached for the phone. "Abdul?" he said, never taking his eyes from her, "come to my rooms, please. Yes, now." He put the telephone down, leaned back against the wall and tucked his hands into his trouser pockets. "Your escort is on the way, Miss Benning. Abdul will escort you down to the curb where the trash is usually left."

Enough was enough. Amanda's composure dissolved in a burst of temper. She gave a shriek and flew at him, but Nick caught her shoulders, held her at arm's length.

"You rat," she said, her breath hitching. "You—you skunk! You horrible, hideous savage—"

"What did you call me?"

"You heard me. You're a skunk. A rat. A—"

"A savage." He swung her around, pinned her to the wall. The memory, so long repressed, burst free. "Damn you," he growled. "You're Dawn's roommate."

"Her immoral, American roommate," Amanda said, and showed her teeth. "How brilliant of you to have finally figured it out. But then, I never expected a baboon to have much of a brain."

The door swung open. Dawn al Rashid stepped into the

room. She stared at her shirtless brother, her red-faced best friend, and swallowed hard.

"Isn't that nice?" she said carefully. "I see that you two have already met."

CHAPTER FOUR

AMANDA stared at Dawn. Dawn stared back.

"Dawn," Amanda said, "thank God you're here! Your brother—"

"Did you invite this woman into my home?" Nick's icy words overrode Amanda's. He took a step toward his sister and Dawn took a quick step back. "I want an answer."

"You'll get one if you give me a min—"

"Did you invite her?"

"Don't browbeat your sister," Amanda said furiously. "I already told you that she asked me to come here tonight."

"I will do whatever I please with my sister." Nick swung toward Amanda. His face was white with anger. "You take me for a fool at your own risk."

"Only a fool would imagine I'd lie my way into your home. I know it may come as a shock to you, Sheikh Rashid, but I don't give a flying fig about seeing how a despot lives."

"Amanda," Dawn muttered, "take it easy."

"Don't tell me to take it easy!" Amanda glared at the sheikh's sister. "And where have you been? Just go take a look at my brother's rooms and I'll meet you there, you said."

"I know. And I'm sorry. I tore my panty hose, and—"

"It's true, then. You not only invited this person into my home, you told her she was free to invade my private rooms."

"Nick," Dawn said, "you don't understand."

"No," the sheikh snapped, "I don't. That my own sister would think I would welcome into my presence the very woman who corrupted her—"

"How dare you say such things?" Amanda stepped in front of Nick. "I never corrupted anyone. I came here as a favor to your sister, to do a job I really didn't want to do because I already knew what you were like, that you were a horrible man with a swollen ego.''

Her eyes flashed. This was pointless and she knew it. Her rage was almost palpable. She yearned to slap that insufferably smug look from Nicholas al Rashid's face, but he'd never let her get away with it. Instead, she moved around him.

''I'm out of here. Dawn, if your brother, the high-muck-a-muck of the universe, lets you use the phone, give me a call tomorrow. Otherwise—''

Nick's hand closed on her arm. ''You will go nowhere,'' he growled, ''until I have answers to my questions.''

''Dammit,'' Amanda said, gritting her teeth and struggling against his grasp, ''let go of me!''

''When I'm good and ready.''

''You have no right—''

''Oh, for heaven's sake!'' Nick and Amanda looked at Dawn. She was staring at the two of them as if she'd never seen them before. ''What in hell is going on here?''

''Don't curse,'' Nick said sharply.

''Then don't treat me like an imbecile.'' Dawn slapped her hands on her hips and glared. ''Yes, I invited Amanda here tonight.''

''As my 'gift','' Nick said, his mouth twisting.

''That's right. I wanted to give you something special for your birthday.''

''Did you really think I'd find it appealing to have you provide a woman for my entertainment?''

''Holy hell,'' Amanda snarled, ''I was not provided for your entertainment! And don't bother telling me not to curse, Your Dictatorship, because I don't have to take orders from you.''

''I can't imagine what my sister was thinking when she made these arrangements.''

''I'll tell you what your sister was thinking. She thought—''
Dawn slammed her fist against the top of the dresser. ''Why not let *me* tell you what I was thinking?'' she snapped.

''Stay out of this,'' Nick said.

''This is unbelievable. All this fuss because I decided your apartment looked like an ad for the No-Taste Furniture Company!'' Her mouth thinned as she glared at Nick. ''What a mistake I made, fixing you up with the services of an interior designer.''

Nick blinked. ''A what?''

''A designer. Someone trained to figure out how to turn this—this warehouse for overpriced, overdone, overvelveted garbage into a home.''

''Oh, go on,'' Nick said with a tight smile, ''don't hold back. Just tell me what you really think.''

''You know it's the truth.'' Dawn waved her arms in the air. ''This apartment looks more like a—a mortician's showroom than a home. So I called Amanda, who just happens to be one of the city's best-known designers. Isn't that right, Amanda?''

Amanda glanced at the sheikh. He was looking at her, and the expression on his face wasn't encouraging.

''And one of its most modest,'' Dawn added hurriedly. ''She was booked up to her eyeballs. The mayor's mansion. The penthouse in that new building on the river. You know, the one that was written up in *Citylights* a couple of weeks ago.''

''Dawn,'' Amanda said, and cleared her throat, ''I don't think—''

''No. No, you certainly didn't. I didn't think it, either. Who'd imagine my brother would want to turn down such a gift from his favorite sister?''

''My only sister,'' Nick said dryly.

''The gift of a brilliant interior designer,'' Dawn said, ignoring the interruption, ''who made room in her incredibly busy schedule solely as a favor to an old friend...'' She paused dramatically. ''And what have you done to her, Nicky?''

Color slashed Nick's high cheekbones. ''What kind of question is that?''

''A logical one. Just look at her. Her dress is torn. Her hair's a mess. She's missing a shoe—''

"Excuse me," Amanda said. "There's no need to take inventory."

"And you, Nicky." Dawn huffed out a breath. "I had no idea my brother, the Lion of the Desert, was in the habit of conducting business with his shirt off."

Amanda shut her eyes, opened them and looked at the sheikh. The flush along his cheeks had gone from red to crimson.

"I have no need to explain myself to anyone," he said brusquely.

"And a good thing, too, because how you could possibly explain this—"

"But since you're my sister, I'll satisfy your curiosity. We fought over Ms. Benning's spy camera."

"My what?" Amanda laughed. "Honestly, Dawn. This brother of yours—"

Nick's eyes narrowed. "Be careful," he said softly, "before you push me too far."

"Well, you've already pushed *me* too far." Dawn marched to Amanda's side and took her hand. "We'll be in my room, Nicky, when you're ready to apologize."

The sheikh stiffened. The room went still. Even the distant sounds of the party—the strains of music, the buzz of conversation that had begun drifting up the stairs a little while before—seemed to stop.

Amanda sensed that a line had been crossed.

She looked at Dawn, who seemed perfectly calm—but the grip of her hand was almost crushing. The women's eyes met. Hang on, Dawn's seemed to say and we can get away with this.

Together, they started for the door. It was like walking away from a stick of dynamite with a lit fuse. One step. Two. Just another few to go—

"An admirable performance, little sister."

Dawn let out her breath. Amanda did, too. She hadn't even realized she'd been holding it. Both of them turned around.

"Nicky," Dawn said softly, "Nicky, if you'd just calm down—"

"Do as you suggested. Take Ms. Benning to your room." His eyes swept over Amanda. She fought back the urge to smooth down her skirt, grasp her torn strap, fix her hair. Instead, she lifted her chin and met his look without blinking. "Give her something to wear. Let her make herself respectable and then bring her downstairs."

"I am not a package to be brought downstairs or anywhere else, for that matter. Who do you think you are, giving orders to your sister about me? If you have something to say to me—"

"The matter is settled for the moment."

"The matter is settled permanently." She tore her hand from Dawn's tight grasp. "I wouldn't so much as pick out the wallpaper for your kitchen, let alone—"

"Get her out of here." Nick waved an imperious hand. He knew he sounded like an ass, but what else was there to do? Dawn's story had holes in it the size of the Grand Canyon. He was angry at her, angry at the Benning woman, but he was furious at himself for losing control in the bed that seemed to loom, stage center, a thousand times larger than life.

What in *hell* had he been thinking, to have almost made love to her?

He hadn't been thinking, he decided grimly. That was the problem. His brain had gone on holiday, thanks to Amanda Benning's clever machinations. A far more dangerous part of his anatomy had taken over.

But his thought processes were clear now. He wasn't about to let this situation deteriorate any further, nor was he about to permit Amanda to walk away before he was certain of what she'd been up to.

"Go on," he said to his sister. "Get her out of here and I'll deal with you both when the night ends."

"Deal with us?" Amanda's voice rose. "You'll deal with us?"

"Oh, he doesn't really mean—"

"Silence!"

The command roared through the room. Amanda caught her breath. She'd never heard a man speak to a woman that way. Her own father had been strict, her stepfather could be crude, and her ex had specialized in sarcasm, but this was different. Nicholas al Rashid's voice carried the ring of absolute authority. Shirtless and disheveled, there was still no mistaking the raw power that emanated from him.

She looked at Dawn and waited for her to respond, to stand up to her brother and tell him that she didn't have to take orders.

To her horror Dawn bowed her head. "Yes, my lord," she whispered.

Amanda stepped in front of her friend. "Now wait just a minute—"

"As for you," Nick barked, "you will speak only when spoken to."

"Listen here, you—you pathetic stand-in for a real human being—"

Nick grabbed her by the elbows and hoisted her to her toes. "Watch how you speak to me."

"Watch how you speak to *me*, Your Horribleness. You might have your sister bowing and scraping like a slave, but not me!"

"Mandy," Dawn pleaded, "stay out of this. Let me explain—"

"Yes," Nick said. He let go of Amanda and folded his arms. "Do that. Now that I think about it, why should I wait until later for an explanation? Explain to me why I found your so-called friend, your interior designer, taking photographs of my things with a spy camera."

"I told you, it wasn't a spy camera."

"It was designed to be concealed."

"It was designed to fit inside a pocket or a purse!"

Nick gave a cold smile. "Exactly."

"It was *not* a spy camera, and if you hadn't stomped it into pieces, I could prove it!"

"You will learn to speak when spoken to," he growled. "And if you cannot manage that, I'll lock you away until I've finished with my sister. Do you understand?"

Amanda's heart bounced into her throat. He would do it, too. She could see it in his eyes.

"You're despicable," she said in a choked whisper. "How I could ever have let you—"

Nick said something in a language she didn't understand. She shrieked as he picked her up, slung her over his shoulder and strode toward a large walk-in closet.

"Put me down. Damn you, put me—"

He yanked the door open, dumped her inside the closet. She dived for the door, but she was too late. It shut in her face, and then she heard a scraping sound against the wood. Amanda rattled the knob, pounded her fist against the door until she was panting, but it was useless.

The sheikh must have jammed a chair under the doorknob. She was trapped.

All she could do was listen to the murmur of voices. The sheikh's angry, Dawn's apologetic. After a while, she couldn't hear anything, not even a whisper. She could imagine Dawn, cowed into submission, while her abominable brother stood over her, glowering. Glowering was what he seemed to do best.

"Bastard," Amanda said softly.

Tears welled in her eyes. Tears of anger.

"Oh, hell," she whispered. Who was she kidding? They were tears of shame. Her rage at the sheikh's accusations, at what he'd done to her camera, at how he'd treated her, was nothing compared to the rage she felt at herself.

How could she have kissed him? Because she had kissed him; she'd have done more than that if she hadn't mercifully come to her senses just before Dawn came into the room. She'd lost control of herself in Nicholas al Rashid's arms. Done things. Said things. Felt things...

Let go, her husband used to say. *What's the matter with you? Why are you such a prude when it comes to sex?*

Well, she hadn't been a prude tonight. She'd behaved as if she were exactly what the sheikh had accused her of being.

"Oh, hell," Amanda said again, and she leaned back, slid to the floor, wrapped her arms around her knees and settled in to wait until His Royal Highness, the Despot of Quidar, deigned to set her free.

It wasn't a very long wait. But when the door opened, it wasn't the despot who stood outside. It was Dawn.

Amanda scrambled to her feet. "What happened?"

"Nick is furious."

"Not half as furious as I am." She peered past Dawn. "Where is he? I haven't finished telling him what—"

"He took his stuff and went to one of the guest rooms to change." Dawn glanced at the diamond watch on her wrist. "By now, he's probably downstairs."

"Yeah, well then, that's where I'm—"

"Mandy." Dawn caught Amanda's hand. "What happened before I got here?"

Color swept into Amanda's face. "Nothing happened," she said, and wrenched her hand free. She smoothed down her dress, tugged uselessly at the torn strap and wished she knew what had happened to her other shoe. "Your brother caught me in here and jumped to all the wrong conclusions."

"Uh-huh." Dawn managed a smile. "So he thought I'd arranged a gift for his, uh, for his pleasure?"

"He most certainly did. As if I'd ever—"

"I know. Sometimes it's not easy dealing with Nicky."

"That's because his head is as hard as a rock."

"Do us both a favor, okay? Don't say things like that to him. You can't call him names, not when he's angry. It isn't done."

"Maybe not in your country, but this is America." Amanda hobbled past Dawn, eyes on the carpet as she searched for her shoe. "Freedom of speech, remember? The Bill of Rights? The Constitution? Ah. There it is." She bent down, picked up her shoe and grimaced. "The heel is broken. Okay, okay,

that's it. Tell your brother he owes me for the camera and now
for a pair of shoes.''

"One dress, too, from the looks of it." Dawn hesitated.
"You guys must have really tussled over that camera."

Amanda was glad she had her back to Dawn. "Yes. Yes,
we did."

"The thing is, I never figured you'd get caught alone in his
bedroom. I was sure I'd get here before he came home."

"Well, you didn't." Amanda heard the sharpness in her
own voice. She stopped, drew a breath and turned around.
"Look, what happened isn't your fault. Anyway, now that
your brother knows the truth—"

"Well, he's not sure he does."

"You mean he still thinks you arranged for me to—"

"No. No, not that." Dawn sat down on the edge of the bed,
sighed and crossed her legs. "Mandy, try to see things from
his perspective. I mean, you saw that awful photograph on the
cover of *Gossip*. People try to get close to him all the time
just so they can find out personal stuff about his life."

"I'd sooner get close to a python."

"I know how you feel. But Nick is sensitive about invasions
of his privacy."

"Your brother is about as sensitive as a mule. And you
know damn well that I wasn't invading anything."

"Of course. And he'll know it, too." Dawn blew out her
breath. "Just as soon as the party is over."

"Yeah, well, you can explain it to him by yourself."
Amanda slung her evening purse over her shoulder and limped
to the door. "Because I am out of here."

"You can't."

"Oh, but I can." She looked back as she curled her hand
around the knob. "I feel sorry for you, Dawn. You're trapped
with His Arrogance, but I'm... Dammit! This—door—is—
stuck!" Dawn said something so quietly that Amanda couldn't
hear it. "What?" she said, and rattled the knob again.

"I said, the door isn't stuck. It's locked."

Amanda stood perfectly still. When she let go of the knob

and looked around, her face was a study in disbelief. "From the outside?"

"Uh-huh." Dawn swung her foot back and forth. She seemed to be contemplating her black silk pump. "I guess some nutcase owned this penthouse before Nicky did. Lots of the doors have locks on the——"

"I don't care who owned it, dammit!"

"I'm just explaining…" Dawn licked her lips. "Nicky locked the door."

"Nicky locked…" Amanda clamped her lips together. Be calm, she told herself, be very calm. "Let me understand this. Your brother locked this door the same way he locked me into the closet?"

Dawn peered intently at her shoes. "Right."

"And you let him do it?"

"I didn't *let* him do anything." Dawn looked up. "He just did it. He has the right." Amanda laughed. Dawn's face pinkened. "Mandy," she said, "I know this seems strange to you——"

"Strange? Strange, that a man I hardly know doesn't think twice about locking me up?" Amanda grabbed for her dangling shoulder strap. "That he feels free to try to rip my clothes off? To tumble me into his bed?"

A grin, a real one, curled across Dawn's mouth. "Oh, wow," she said softly. "So that wasn't true, huh? Nicky's little speech about losing his shirt when you were fighting over the camera."

"The truth," Amanda said stiffly, "is that your dear, devoted brother is a lunatic. And so are you, for letting him lock that door."

Dawn shot to her feet. "I didn't 'let' him. I told you that. Nobody 'lets' him, don't you see? My brother is the future ruler of our kingdom. His word is law."

"For you, maybe. And for anybody else who's willing to live in the Dark Ages."

"Now, you just wait a minute before you say——"

The door suddenly swung open. Amanda spun around and glared at the man she despised.

How calm and collected he looked. While she'd been cooling her heels behind locked doors, the Sheikh of the Universe had been readying himself for his party. His dark hair was still damp from the shower; his jaw was smooth. She could see a tiny cut in the shallow cleft in his chin.

Good, she thought grimly. Maybe he wasn't as calm as he looked. The son of a bitch had cut himself while he shaved. She only hoped she was the reason for his unsteady hand on the razor. From the way he'd looked at her before and from how he was looking at her now, it was pretty obvious that Nicholas al Rashid wasn't accustomed to having anyone, especially a woman, talk back to him.

Women probably told him lots of other things, though. That he was exciting. That he was gorgeous, especially in that tux and pleated white shirt. That he could make a woman forget everything, even the code she lived by, with one kiss....

Amanda drew herself up. Snakes could be handsome, too. That didn't make them any less repulsive.

"You have one hell of a nerve," she said, "locking us in this room."

Nick looked at his sister. "Dawn?"

"This is the United States of America in case you haven't—"

"Dawn, our guests are here."

Amanda strode toward him. "Are you deaf?" Her words were rimed with ice. "I'm talking to you."

Nick ignored her. "Thanks to this unpleasant incident, I am not at the door to greet them."

Dawn cast her eyes down. "It's my fault, Nicholas. I apologize."

"I've decided to forgive you."

A glowing smile lit Dawn's face. "Thank you, Nicky."

Amanda made a little sound of disgust. Nick decided to go on pretending she was invisible.

"But this is the last time. One more transgression and you return home."

"Oh, give me a break."

Dawn shot Amanda a horrified look. Nick merely tilted his head toward her. "Did you have something you wished to say, Ms. Benning?"

"How generous of you to notice."

"Is that a yes?"

Amanda limped toward him. "It is indeed."

Nick looked at his watch, then at her. "Say it, then. I'm in a hurry, thanks to you."

"And I'm out a camera, a dress and a pair of shoes, thanks to you." It wasn't easy to maintain your dignity with one shoe three inches higher than the other, but Amanda was determined to manage it. "I'm going to send you a bill for—" she paused, furiously adding the numbers in her head "—for nine hundred and eighty dollars."

"Really."

Damn him for that annoying little smirk! "Yes," she said with a smirk of her own, "really. That camera was expensive."

"Oh, I'm sure it was." He folded his arms and raked her with a glance, his gaze settling, at last, on her face. "I'm just surprised that your dress and shoes would be so costly, considering what little there was of both."

Actually, Nick thought, that was overstating it. A wisp of red. Two slender straps. A pair of high-heeled sandals that made her legs long and endless...

One sandal. The other was broken, now that he took a closer look. That was the reason she'd lurched toward him. Still, those legs were as long and endless as he'd remembered. As long and glorious as they'd felt, wrapped around him when he'd tumbled her down onto the bed.

The feel of her beneath him. The soft thrust of her breasts. The scent of her hair. The taste of her mouth...

Nick frowned.

Terrific. He'd found a conniving little schemer in his bed-

room, and just remembering what she'd felt like in his arms
was enough to send his hormones into a frenzy.

Disgusted, he walked past her and paused before the mir-
rored wall that faced his bed, supposedly to straighten his tie
when what actually needed straightening was his libido.

What was the matter with him? All right. Amanda Benning
was beautiful. She was as sexy as sin. So what?

All his women were beautiful and sexy, but he hadn't stumbled across any one of them hiding in his bedroom, snapping
photos with a camera that would have made James Bond en-
vious, then coming to life in his arms when she'd decided the
situation was desperate enough to require a distraction.

This was a setup. Nick was positive of it. What else could
it be? His little sister, complaining about the furnishings of his
apartment? It didn't ring true. Dawn never noticed her sur-
roundings unless it was the once-a-year encampment their father demanded of her, and she only noticed then because she
hated the heat, the dust, the inconvenience of sleeping in a
tent.

As for Amanda—if she was an interior designer, then the
moon was made of green cheese. And, dammit, she brought
out the worst in him.

First he'd mauled her. No point in pretending, not to himself. He'd come on to her with the subtlety of a freight train,
and never mind all his rationalizations about playing her game,
or teaching her a lesson, or whatever nonsense he'd used to
justify wanting to kiss her.

Then he'd come to his senses, started to let her go, but
ended up trying to seduce her instead. That didn't make sense,
either. Why would he try to seduce a woman whose motives
for being in his bedroom were, at the very least, questionable?

And then there was the icing on the cake. The way he'd
talked to Dawn, as if he really were the tottering ghost of old
Rudy Valentino. Just thinking about it was humiliating.
Nicholas al Rashid, stepping straight out of an outdated
Hollywood flick, complete with flaring nostrils, attitude, and
macho enough to make a camel gag.

The only thing he'd left out was the shoe-polish hair.

Yeah, he thought, yeah, he'd made a fool of himself.

And for what? Because he'd found Amanda Benning in his bedroom? He'd destroyed her disk, broken her camera. Abdul would give him a report on her in a little while and then he'd put the fear of God in her.

Nick's mouth twitched. The fear of his lawyers, to be specific. One well-worded threat and she'd be out of his life for good.

The world was full of women, lots of them as beautiful as this one. There was nothing special about her. His mouth thinned. There hadn't been anything special about her seven years ago, either, when his panic over Dawn was all that had stood between him and insanity—

"...an itemized bill."

Nick scowled at his reflection, turned and looked at Amanda, who'd come up to stand behind him. "What?"

"I said, I'll send you an itemized bill if you don't believe that I paid almost three hundred dollars for the dress."

"There's no need for that. Abdul—my secretary—will write you a check before you leave tonight."

"Good old Abdul," Amanda said pleasantly. "Still crawling around on his hands and knees, is he?" Her chin lifted. "Tell him to get busy, then, because I'm going straight out the front door the instant I get down—"

"No."

"No? But you just said—"

"You're not leaving so quickly, Ms. Benning."

"On the contrary, Sheikh Rashid. As far as I'm concerned, I'm not leaving quickly enough."

"You will leave here after I'm done with you. Dawn?" Nick smiled. "People are asking for you."

"Oh. But you said—"

"I know what I said. I've changed my mind. I'd prefer not to have to try to explain your absence."

"What's the matter?" Amanda said nastily. "Are you

afraid people might be put off if they knew you were in the habit of locking women in your bedroom?"

The sheikh smiled at his sister. "Just behave yourself."

"Just behave yourself," Amanda said in wicked imitation. "What does that mean? Is she supposed to walk two paces to the rear?"

"Go on." Nick kissed Dawn's cheek. "Go downstairs and tell our guests I've been momentarily detained."

Dawn hesitated. "What about Amanda?"

Nick's smile thinned. "I'll take care of her."

"Dawn?" Amanda said, but Dawn shook her head and hurried out of the room. Abdul seemed to materialize in the doorway.

"There you are, Abdul," Nick said.

"My lord."

"Has it arrived?"

"Yes, my lord."

Nick nodded. Abdul bent down, then straightened up with two elaborately wrapped boxes in his arms.

"On the bed, please."

The little man walked to the bed and put the boxes down. Then he bowed his body in half and backed out of the room.

"Those are for you."

Amanda looked at the things lying on the bed as if they might start ticking.

"A dress," Nick said lazily, "and a pair of shoes."

"Are you crazy?"

"I would be, if I let you slip away without confirming your reasons for being here." He jerked his head at the boxes. "I guessed at your sizes."

"I'm sure you're an expert," she said coldly.

"And," he said, ignoring the taunt, "I did my best to describe the style of your things to the concierge."

"How nice for the concierge." She folded her arms and lifted her chin. "But you should have told her to order them in her size."

"In his size," Nick said with a little smile, "but I doubt if they're quite to his taste."

"Maybe you didn't hear me before, Sheikh Rashid. I said I wanted a check to pay for my things, not replacements."

"And you shall have a check. But I've no intention of letting you go just yet, Ms. Benning. Dawn's things won't fit you. And I certainly won't permit you to insult my guests by moving among them while you look like something no self-respecting cat would drag home."

Amanda's brows rose. "If you honestly think I want to go to your party—"

"I'm not interested in what you think, honestly or otherwise. But I must attend my party, as must my sister. And, since I need to keep you here for another few hours, I have no choice but to subject my guests to your presence."

Heat swept into her face. "You are the most insulting man I've ever had the misfortune to meet."

"Ah, Ms. Benning. That breaks my heart." Nick pointed a commanding finger at the boxes. "Now, take those things into the dressing room. Change your dress and shoes. Fix your hair and do whatever is required to make yourself presentable. Then you will emerge, take my arm, stay at my side all evening, comport yourself with decorum and speak to no one unless I grant permission for you to do so."

"In your dreams!"

"If you do all that, and if your so-called interior design credentials check out, you will be free to leave. If not..."

"If not, what?" Amanda's jaw shot out. "Will you lock me in the dungeon?"

His smile was slow and heart-stopping in its male arrogance. "What a fine idea."

"You—you..."

Nick looked at his watch. "You have five minutes."

"You're a horrible man, Sheikh Rashid!"

"I'm waiting, Ms. Benning." He looked up, his cold silver eyes locked on hers. "Perhaps you require my assistance."

Amanda snatched the boxes from the bed and fled into the

dressing room. Angry tears blinded her as she stripped off her dress and kicked her shoes into a corner. Then she opened the packages and took out what Nick had bought her.

The dress looked almost like the one he'd ruined, except it had surely cost ten times as much and seemed to have been fashioned of cobwebs instead of silk. The shoes were elegant wisps of satin and slid on her feet as if they'd been made for her.

Nick rapped sharply on the door. "One minute."

She looked at herself in the mirror. Her eyes were bright. Her cheeks were pink. With anger, she told herself. Of course with anger. And it was anger, too, that had sent her heart leaping into her throat.

She ran her fingers through her hair, bit her lips to color them. Then she threw back her head, unlocked the door and stepped into the bedroom.

Nick was leaning back against the wall, arms folded, feet crossed at the ankles. He gave her a long, appraising look, from the top of her head to her feet, then up again. "I take it the dress and shoes fit."

His tone was polite, but when his eyes met hers, they were shot with silver fire. She could feel the heat swirling in her blood.

"I despise you," she said in a voice that sounded far too breathless.

He uncoiled his body like a lazy cat and came toward her. "Liking me isn't a prerequisite for the night we're about to spend together."

"We aren't," she said quickly, even though she knew he was baiting her, that he was really just referring to the time she'd be with him at his party. "There's no way in hell I'd spend the night with—"

He bent and brushed his mouth over hers. That was all he did; the kiss was little more than a whisper of flesh to flesh, but the intake of her breath more than proved she was lying.

She knew it. He knew it. And she hated him for it.

"The Sheikh," she said, her eyes cool.

"I beg your pardon?"

"*The Sheikh,* starring Rudolph Valentino. It's an old movie. You'd love it. Be sure and rent the video sometime."

Nick laughed. "I can see we're going to have a delightful evening." He held out his arm. She tossed her head. "Take it," he said softly, "unless you'd rather I lift you into my arms and carry you."

Amanda took his arm. She could feel the hardness of his muscles, the taut power of his body through his clothing—but mostly, she could feel the race of her own heart as he led her out of his bedroom and to the wide staircase that led downstairs.

CHAPTER FIVE

AMANDA knew all about making an entrance.

Her father, a California businessman who owned a department store and had hopes of building it into a chain, had put his three beautiful little daughters in front of the cameras whenever he could. They'd promoted everything from baby clothes to barbecue grills.

"Lick your lips, girls," he'd say just before he'd walk them out. "And give 'em a big smile."

The small-town lawyer she'd married had turned into a publicity-hungry politico looking for national office before she'd had time to blink.

"Smile," he'd say, and he'd put his arm around her waist as if he really cared, just before walking her into a room filled with strangers.

Her stepfather, Jonas Baron, was the exception. Jonas owned almost half of Texas but he didn't much care about entrances or exits. He never sought public attention but he couldn't escape it, either.

Still, nothing could have prepared her for what it was like to make an entrance on the arm of the Lord of the Desert.

"Oh, hell," Nick said softly when they reached the top of the stairs.

Oh, hell, indeed, Amanda thought as she looked down.

A million faces looked back. And oh, the expressions on those faces! All those eyes, shifting with curiosity from the sheikh to her...

She jerked to a stop. "Everyone is watching us," she hissed.

"Yeah." Nick cleared his throat. "I should have realized this might happen. It's because I'm late."

"Well, that's not my fault!"

"Of course it's your fault," he growled.

"I'm not going down there. Not with you."

Nick must have anticipated that she'd move away because his free hand shot out and covered hers as it lay on his arm. To the people watching, it would have looked like a courtly gesture, but the truth was that his hand felt like a shackle on hers.

"Don't be ridiculous. They've all seen us. As it is, tongues will wag. If you run off now, there'll be no stopping the stories."

"That's your problem, Lord Rashid, not mine."

He looked at her, his eyes narrowed and hard. "You're my sister's oldest friend." Slowly, he began descending the steps with Amanda locked to his side. "And you've come to pay her a visit."

"I'm the immoral creature who led her astray. Isn't that what you mean?"

"You haven't seen each other in ages, not since—when?"

She looked at him. His mouth was set in a polite smile.

"How charming," she said coolly. "You can speak without moving your lips."

"When did you and Dawn last see each other?"

"Two weeks ago, at lunch. Not exactly 'ages', is it?"

Nick's hand tightened over hers. "Just keep your story straight. You're Dawn's friend. You've kept in touch over the years. She heard you were in town and invited you to her birthday party."

They were halfway down the steps. Amanda looked at all those upturned faces. The only thing lacking was a trumpet fanfare, she thought, and bit back a hysterical bark of laughter.

"Did you hear me, Ms. Benning?"

"I heard you, Lord Rashid. But I'm not visiting New York. I live here. I know you'd prefer to think I live in Casablanca and that I'm a spy."

"What I think, Ms. Benning, is that you watch too many old movies."

"What am I supposed to say if people ask why you and I came downstairs together?"

It was, Nick decided, an excellent question. "Tell them...tell them I hadn't seen you in a long time."

"Not long enough," Amanda said, smiling through her teeth.

"You and I were catching up on old times."

"Ah. Is that some quaint Quidaran idiom that means you were trying to jump my bones?"

Nick stopped so abruptly that she stumbled. He caught her, his arm looping tightly around her waist.

"Listen to me," he growled. "You are to behave yourself. You will smile pleasantly, say the proper thing at the proper moment. And if you don't—"

"Don't threaten me, Lord Rashid. I'll behave, but not because I'm afraid of you. It's because I've no desire for ugly publicity."

"Afraid it might ruin your image?" he said sarcastically.

"Being seen with you will be enough to do— What are they doing?"

The question was pointless. She could see, and hear, what all those people down there were doing. They were applauding.

"They're applauding," Amanda said, and looked at him.

Nick gave her a smile so phony she wondered if it made his mouth hurt.

"I know."

"Well, why are they—"

"The applause is for me."

She looked down again, into that sea of smiling faces, at the clapping hands. Then she looked at Nick. Definitely, that smile had to be painful.

"They're clapping for you?" she said incredulously.

"Must I repeat myself?" A muscle tightened in his cheek. "It is the custom."

"The custom?"

"Do you think you're capable of making a statement, Ms.

Benning, instead of following each question with another? Yes. It is the custom to applaud the prince on his birthday."

"Well, it's dumb."

Nick laughed. Really laughed. "It is indeed."

"Then why do you permit it?"

He thought of a hundred different answers, starting with three thousand years of history and ending with the knowledge that had come to him only after more than a decade of trying to push his country into the twenty-first century—the simple realization that not even he could accomplish such a thing quickly.

He could tell Amanda Benning all of that, but why should he? She wouldn't understand. And the odds were excellent that if he did, she'd rush to sell that morsel of news to the highest bidder.

As it was, he was doing everything possible not to think about her trying to sell the sordid little tale of what had gone on in his bedroom. Surely his lawyers' threats would stop her. And if that didn't do the trick, he'd deny whatever she said. But would he be able to deny the memory of those moments to himself? The feel of her in his arms? The taste of her on his tongue?

Of course he would, he thought calmly.

"I permit the applause," he said, "because it is the custom."

"That's ridiculous."

"We have other customs you would probably call ridiculous, as well, including one that demands a woman's silence in my presence until I grant her permission to speak."

"Is that a threat?"

"It's a promise."

Amanda shook her head in disbelief. "I have no idea how Dawn tolerates you."

"And I have no idea how someone like you managed to insinuate yourself into my sister's life. Now, smile and behave yourself."

"You're a horrible man, Lord Rashid."

"Thank you for the compliment, Ms. Benning."

They reached the bottom of the steps. Nick smiled. So did Amanda. The crowd surged forward and swallowed them up.

An hour later, Nick was still leading Amanda from guest to guest.

If her ex could only see her now, she thought wryly.

Not wanting to be stage center was one of the first things they'd quarreled over, but that was where she'd been all evening. If there'd been a spotlight in the room, it would have been beamed at her head.

Nicholas al Rashid might be the Lord of the Realm, the Lion of the Desert, the Heir to the Imperial Throne and the Wizard of Oz, but not even he could control people's tongues. And those tongues were all wagging. Wagging, Amanda thought grimly, at top speed.

"My sister's friend," he said each time he introduced her. "Ms. Amanda Benning."

The answers hardly varied. "Oh," people said, "how...interesting."

She knew that what they really wanted to say was that if she was Dawn's friend, why had she made such a spectacular entrance on his arm, with no Dawn in sight? For that matter, where was Dawn now?

On the other side of the room, that was where. Dawn had smiled and waggled her fingers, but clearly, she was going to adhere to the rules and keep her distance.

As Nick was walking her toward another little knot of people, Amanda snagged a glass of wine from a waiter and took a sip.

Rules. The sheikh was full of rules. And, fool that he was, he seemed to think people abided by them.

"You see?" he'd said smugly, after he'd marched her around for a while. "No one's asking any questions. It wouldn't be polite."

Idiot, Amanda thought, and took another mouthful of wine. Etiquette could keep people from *saying* what they were

thinking, but nothing could stop the thoughts themselves or
the buzz of speculation that followed them around the room.

Finally, she'd had her fill.

"I don't like this," she murmured. "Everyone is talking
about me."

"You should have thought of that possibility before you
sneaked into my bedroom. Keep moving, please, Ms.
Benning."

"They think I'm your—your—"

"Probably." Nick's jaw knotted; his hand clasped her elbow more tightly as he steered her toward the terrace door.
"That's why it's important to show no reaction to the whispers."

"There isn't anything to whisper about," Amanda said
crossly. "Can't you tell them that?"

Nick laughed.

"I'm glad you find this so amusing." She yanked her arm
free of his hand as they stepped into the cool night air. "Can't
you tell them—"

"Sire?"

Amanda looked over her shoulder. Abdul, looking more like
a pretzel than a man, came hurrying toward them.

"Your slave approacheth," she said, "O Emperor of the
World."

Nick ignored her as Abdul dropped to one knee. "What is
it, Abdul?"

The old man lifted his head just enough to give her a mean-
ingful look. Nick sighed, eased his secretary to his feet and
led him a short distance away. He bent his head, listened, then
nodded.

"Thank you, Abdul."

"My lord," Abdul said, and shuffled backward into the living room.

"He's too old to be doing that whenever he comes near
you."

"I agree. But—"

"Don't tell me. It's the custom, right? And we wouldn't

want to ignore the custom even if it means that poor little man has to keep banging his knees against the floor.''

Nick's jaw shot forward. ''Abdul was my father's secretary. He was my grandfather's apprentice clerk. This is the way he's always done things, the way he expects to do...'' He stopped talking. Amanda was looking at him as if he were some alien species of life. ''Never mind,'' he said coldly. ''I'm not going to spend the evening in debate.''

''Of course not, because you know you'd lose.''

''What I know,'' Nick said even more coldly, ''is that Abdul's just reminded me of some things that need my attention. You're on your own.''

Amanda raised her hands and flexed her wrists. ''Off with the handcuffs,'' she said brightly.

''You're to keep away from Dawn.''

''Certainly, sire.''

''You're not to bother anyone with personal questions.''

''Darn,'' she cooed, batting her lashes. ''And here I was, hoping to ask the governor what he wore to bed.''

''Other than that, you're free to move among my guests unattended.''

''Does that mean I passed the background check?''

''It means I'm too busy to go on playing baby-sitter, and that if you try to leave before I'm done with you, you'll be stopped by my security people.''

''How gracious of you, Lord Rashid.''

Nick flashed a grim smile. ''What man would not wish to be gracious to you, Ms. Benning?'' he answered, and strolled back into the brightly lit living room.

''Good riddance,'' Amanda muttered, watching him.

''Nicky!''

He was halfway across the room when Deanna Burgess launched herself into the sheikh's arms. Amanda's eyebrows lifted. It was a warm greeting, to say the least, but the look she shot over his shoulder was far from warm.

Obviously, Deanna Burgess knew Nick had made his entrance with her on his arm. Of course she knew, Amanda thought grimly. She drank some more wine. Two hundred and fifty absolute strangers had witnessed that entrance and the odds were excellent that most of them were still talking about it.

Oh, if only she could get that sort of publicity for Benning Designs.

Amanda lifted her glass to her mouth. It was empty. She tilted it up and let the last golden drops trickle onto her tongue. Time for another drink, she thought, and strolled into the living room.

There had to be a way to turn this disaster into something useful. Dawn's original plan certainly wasn't going to work now. No way would the sheikh agree to let Benning Designs decorate the penthouse.

Amanda smiled at the bartender, put down her empty glass and exchanged it for a full one.

Think, she told herself, think. What would Paul do? Her ex, with his toothpaste smile, had been unsurpassed at turning political liabilities into political bonuses.

She took a drink. Mmm. The wine was delicious. And cooling.

Jonas, then. Her stepfather was the sort of man who'd never let a difficult situation stop him. What would Jonas do?

"...old friend, or so he..."

The whispered buzz sounded as clearly as a bell in the seconds it took the chamber quartet to segue from Vivaldi to Mozart. The little knot of people that had produced it looked at her. Amanda looked back, lifted her glass. One man colored and lifted his, too.

The bastards were, indeed, talking about her.

She buried her frown in her glass.

If only they'd talk about Benning Designs instead of Amanda Benning, but there was no way that would happen. Not even Jonas Baron could turn this silk purse into a sow's ear. Or maybe it was the other way around. Even old Jonas would be helpless in this situation. The best he'd do would be to come up with some creaky saying.

Like, you had to roll with the punches. Like, those were the breaks. Like, when life hands you lemons...

"Make lemonade," Amanda said, and blinked.

"Sorry?"

She swung around, gave the bartender a big smile. "I said, could I have another glass of wine, please?"

Glass in hand, smiling brilliantly, she headed straight for the little group of whisperers.

"Hello," she said, and stuck out her hand. "I'm Amanda Benning. Of Benning Designs. I apologize for making His Highness late for his own party, but I had him all excited." She smiled modestly and wondered if the woman to her left knew her mouth was hanging open. "He's so private, you know."

"Oh," the woman with the hanging jaw said, "we know!"

"He probably thought it would upset me if he told anyone what we'd really been doing upstairs."

Four mouths opened. Four heads leaned toward her. Amanda tried not to laugh.

"I'd just shown him some fabric swatches, and he—Nicky—well, he just loved them." She did laugh this time, but in a way that made it clear she was sharing a charming anecdote with her new acquaintances. "And then he wanted to see some paint chips, and before we knew it, the time had just flown by."

Silence. She knew what was happening. She hoped she did anyway. The little group of guests was processing what she'd said. Come on, she thought impatiently, come on! Surely one of you wants to be first—

"You mean," the man who'd had the decency to blush said, "you're the sheikh's interior decorator?"

"His interior designer." Amanda smiled so hard her lips ached. "And I can hardly wait to get started. I had to shift my calendar around to make room for the sheikh—"

"Really."

"Yes. Really." Amanda curled her free hand around the slender shoulder strap of her evening purse and hoped nobody could see her crossed fingers. "The vice president will be a bit put out, I know, but, well, when the Lion of the Desert makes a request—"

"The vice president? And the sheikh?" The woman with the drooping jaw was almost drooling as she leaned closer. "Isn't it funny? That you should mention interior decorating, I mean?"

"Design," Amanda said, and smiled politely.

"Oh. Of course. But what I meant is, we've been thinking of redoing our cottage in the Hamptons."

Amanda arched a brow. A cottage in the Hamptons. She knew what that meant. A dozen rooms, minimum. Or maybe fifty.

"Really," she said with what she hoped was the right mix of politeness and boredom. "How nice."

A waiter floated by with a tray of champagne. She grabbed his elbow, swapped her now empty glass for a flute of bubbly and took a drink. Her head felt light. Well, why wouldn't it? She hadn't eaten in hours.

"I wonder, Ms Benning...would you have time to fit us in?"

Thank you, God. Amanda frowned. "I don't know. My schedule—"

"We'd be grateful if you could just come out and take a look."

"Well, since you're friends of the sheikh—"

"Old friends," the woman said quickly.

"In that case..." Amanda opened her evening purse and whipped out a business card. "Why don't you phone me on Monday?"

"Oh, that would be wonderful."

Wonderful didn't quite do it. Incredible was more like it. She fought back the desire to pump her fist into the air, made a bit more small talk and moved on to the next group of guests.

Before long, her cards were almost all gone. Everybody seemed to want one now that they knew she was Amanda

Benning, the sheikh's designer. It wasn't a lie. Not exactly. She'd have been his designer if Dawn's plan hadn't backfired.

"Ms. Benning," someone called.

Amanda smiled, relieved a waiter of another flute of champagne and started toward the voice. Whoa. The floor was tilting. She giggled softly. You'd think a zillion-billion-million-dollar penthouse wouldn't have warped—

"Amanda."

A pair of strong hands closed on her shoulders. She looked up as Nick stepped in front of her. Wow. His head was tilting, too.

"Are you enjoying yourself?"

How come he wasn't smiling? Amanda gave him a loopy grin. "How 'bout you, Nicky? Are you envoy—enboy—enjoying you'self?" she said, and hiccuped.

Nick marched her through the room, out the door and onto the terrace. It wasn't deserted as it had been before. He clutched her elbow, kept her tightly at his side as he walked her past little clusters of guests.

"Hello," he kept saying. "Having a good time?"

"Hello," Amanda sang happily. "Havin' a goo' time?"

Someone laughed. Nick laughed, too, but his laughter died once they turned the corner of the terrace. "Just what do you think you're doing?" he demanded in a furious whisper.

Amanda blinked owlishly. It was darker out here. She couldn't see Nick's face clearly, but she didn't have to. He was angry, angry that she'd finally been having fun.

"Half my guests are marching around, clutching your address and phone number."

She giggled. "Only half?" Champagne sloshed over the edge of her glass as she raised it to her lips. "Jus' let me finish this and I'll— Hey," she said indignantly as he snatched the flute from her hand. "Give me that."

"Who told you that you could hand out business cards?"

"Who *told* me? Nobody told me. I didn't ask. I wouldn't ask! People don't need permission to hand out business cards."

"They do when they're in my home."

"Tha's ridiculous."

"I won't have you bothering my guests."

"Oh, for goodness' sake, I wasn't bothering anybody." She laughed slyly. "Matter of fact, your guests are eager to meet me."

"I'll bet they are."

"Ever'body wants the sheikh's designer to do their house."

"You're not my designer," he said coldly. "And as soon as they realize that, your little scheme will collapse."

"A minor teshnic—technic—a minor inconvenience."

Nick's eyes narrowed. "And you're drunk."

"I'm not."

"You are."

"No, I'm not," she said, and hiccuped again.

"Have you eaten anything tonight?"

"No."

"Why not?"

Amanda lifted her chin. "I was too busy drinking wine."

Nick said something under his breath. She looked at him.

"Was that Quidaran again? Must have been. I couldn't understand it."

"Be glad you didn't," he said, his voice grim. "Let's go, Ms. Benning."

"Go where?"

"You need a pot of strong coffee and a plate of food."

The mention of food made her stomach lurch. "No. I'm not hungry."

"Coffee, then. And something for your head before it starts to ache."

"Why should it…?" She caught her breath. "Ow," she whispered, and put the back of her hand to her forehead. "My head hurts."

"Indeed." Nick pulled her into the circle of his arm and led her to the end of the terrace.

"Is that a door?"

"That's what it is. Let me punch in the code."

The door swung open. Amanda took a step and faltered. Nick lifted her into his arms, carried her inside, kicked the door shut and switched on the light. She threw her arm over her eyes. "Agh. That's so bright."

"I'll turn it down. Okay. Sit here. And don't move."

She sat. It didn't help. Her head spun. Or the room spun. Either way, she felt awful.

"Nick?"

"Here I am. Open your mouth."

She opened an eye instead. He was holding out a glass and four tablets.

"What's that?"

"I know you'd like to think it's poison, but it's only water and something that'll make your head feel better."

"How about my stomach?" she said in a whisper.

Nick grinned. "That, too. Go on. Take them."

She took the tablets and gave them a wary look. "Are they from Quidar?"

Nick didn't just grin, he laughed. "They're from a pharmacy in Bond Street. Come on. Swallow them down."

She did. He took the glass from her.

"Now, put your feet up." His voice sounded far away, but he was right there, beside her. She could feel his hands, lifting her. Shifting her so her head was propped on something. A bed? A pillow?

His lap.

"Where are we?" she mumbled, and opened one eye.

"My study," Nick said.

The room was small, with an interior door that she assumed led into the rest of the penthouse. It was cozy, she thought. Everything looked lived in: the threadbare old rug, the battered leather sofa and the equally battered desk.

"Dawn didn't show me this."

"No." His voice hummed with amusement. "She doesn't have the combination, so it wouldn't have been on the dollar tour. Shut your eyes and let the tablets do their job."

She did. For five minutes. For an hour. Time passed; she

had no idea how long she lay there. A hand stroked her forehead and she sighed and turned her face into it.

A knock sounded at the door.

Nick lifted her head gently from his lap. She lay back, eyes closed, heard a door open, heard him say, "Thank you," heard the door swing shut.

"Coffee," Nick said. "Freshly ground and brewed."

"It's wonderful to be king," Amanda murmured.

"Wonderful," he said dryly. "Can you sit up?"

She did. He held out an enormous mug, filled to the brim with liquid so black it looked like ink.

She took it, held it in both hands. "It's hot."

"Clever of you to figure that out."

"It's black."

"Clever again."

"I like cream and sugar in my coffee."

"Drink it," he said, "or I'll grab your nose and pour it into your mouth."

He looked as if he might do just that. Amanda drank, shuddered, and drank again. When the cup was empty, she gave it to him. He refilled it, looked at her, sighed and put it down on the desk. Then he took a chair, turned it backward, straddled it and sat.

"Better?"

"Yes." Amazingly, it was true. "What was in those tablets?"

Nick smiled. "You'll have to let me take you to London to find out."

The words were as teasing as his smile, but they made her breath catch.

"You're not being a tyrant," she said.

"It's late, and I'm tired. It takes too much energy to be a tyrant twenty-four hours a day." He folded his arms along the back of the chair, propped his chin on his wrists. "Abdul finished checking you out."

"Ah. Am I Mata Hari?"

"He says you live alone."

Amanda sighed, shut her eyes and laid her head back. "He's a genius."

"He says you're divorced."

She put her index finger to her mouth, licked it, then checked an imaginary scorecard in the air.

"Why?"

Amanda's eyes popped open. "Why what?"

"Why are you divorced?"

"That's none of your business."

"You made everything about you my business when you crept into my room and started taking photographs."

"God, are we back to that? I told you—"

"You were getting data so you could redo my apartment." He reached down, picked up her foot. Amanda tried to jerk it back.

"What are you doing?"

"Taking off your shoes." His hands were gentle though the tips of his fingers felt callused. Why would a sheikh who never did anything except order people around have callused fingers? she wondered dreamily, and closed her eyes as he began massaging her arch.

"Mmm."

"Mmm, indeed." Nick cleared his throat. What in hell was he doing? Well, he wasn't a complete idiot. He *knew* what he was doing; he was sitting in the one room in the overblown, overfurnished, overeverythinged penthouse that really belonged to him with a woman's foot in his lap. And he was thinking something insane. Something totally, completely crazy.

He let go of Amanda's foot, shoved back his chair and stood up.

"You didn't do the mayor's mansion."

Amanda opened her eyes. "No," she said wearily. "I didn't do that penthouse, either."

"Then why did you lie?"

"Dawn lied, not me. I'm a designer, but not the way she said."

"Meaning?"

"Meaning, I've never had a real client."

Abdul had said as much. "Not one?"

"Not unless you count my mother. And my stepbrother. But I'm a good designer. Damned good."

"Don't curse," Nick said mildly. "It isn't feminine."

"Is it feminine for a woman to curl around a man like a vine?"

"What?"

"Deanna Whosis. The woman in that magazine photo. I couldn't tell if she was trying to strangle you or say hello."

Nick grinned, hitched a hip onto the edge of the desk and folded his arms. "You're still tipsy, Ms. Benning."

"I'm cold sober." But if she was, why would she have asked him such a question? "She did it again tonight, too. She seems to think two objects can be in the same space at the same time."

"Jealous?" Nick said with a little smile.

"Why on earth would I be?"

"Maybe because it's a feminine trait."

"You haven't answered my question."

"You haven't really asked one."

"I did."

"You didn't. You asked me about vines and the laws of physics, but what you really want to know is if I'm involved with Deanna."

"I didn't ask you that."

"You didn't have to. And the answer is no, I'm not. Not anymore."

The answer surprised her. "But I saw—"

"I know what you saw. And I'm telling you, Deanna Burgess is history."

Amanda licked her lips. "As of when?" she said softly, and held her breath, waiting for the answer.

"As of the minute I kissed you tonight," Nick said, and as he did, he knew it was the truth.

Amanda stared at him. Then she got to her feet. "It's late," she said, because it was all she could think of to say. Had he really gotten rid of Deanna Burgess because of her? No. The idea was preposterous. It was crazy.

Mostly, it was incredibly exciting.

Nick rose, too. "Deanna is gone, Amanda. From my home and from my life."

"I don't—I don't know why you're telling me this."

"Yes, you do." He put his hand under her chin and tilted her face up. "And I know why you asked."

"I don't know what you're…" Her breath hitched. He was moving his thumb gently over her mouth, tracing its contours. "Nick?"

"I like the way you say my name."

He bent his head, his eyes locked to hers and followed the path his thumb had taken with his lips.

"Kiss me," he said in a rough whisper. "Kiss me the way you did before."

"No," she said, and thrust her hands into his hair, pulled his head down to hers and kissed him.

Moments later, centuries later, she shuddered and pulled back.

"I didn't come here for this."

"No." Nick bent his head, pressed his open mouth to the pulse racing in the hollow of her throat. "Neither did I."

"Nick." She put her hands on his chest to push him away. Instead, her fingers curled into the lapels of his tux. "I'm not a woman who sleeps around."

"That's fine. Because I'm not a man who believes in sharing."

"And I'm not looking for a relationship. My divorce wasn't pleasant. Neither was my marriage. It will be a long, long time before I get involved with another—"

Nick kissed her again, his mouth open and hot. She moaned, swayed, and his arms went around her.

"My life is planned," she whispered. "I was my father's devoted daughter, my mother's rock, my husband's puppet."

"I don't want any of that from you."

"What do you want, then?"

He took her face in his hands. "I want you to be my mistress."

CHAPTER SIX

IT WAS, she realized, a joke.

A bad joke, but a joke all the same. What else could it be?

A man she hardly knew, a man she'd done nothing but argue with, had just told her that he wanted her to be his mistress. He'd said it—no, he'd announced it—with certainty, as if it were an arrangement they'd discussed and agreed to.

A joke, absolutely. Or a sign of insanity…but was what the sheikh had said any more insane than what she'd been doing? Kissing him. Hanging on to him. Aching for him, this rude, self-important stranger…

This gorgeous, sexy, incredible man who'd held her gently when she felt ill.

Amanda's head whirled. She stepped back, tugged down her skirt, smoothed a shaking hand over her hair. Homey little gestures, all of them. Well, who knew?

Maybe they'd restore her equilibrium.

Or maybe she'd misunderstood him. That was possible. After all, just a little while ago, she'd felt as if a crazed tap dancer was loose inside her skull. Could a headache make you hear voices? Could it leave you suffering from delusions?

Was she crazy, or was he?

"Amanda?"

She looked up. Nick's face gave nothing away. He looked like a man waiting for a train. Calm. Cool. Collected. Surely he wouldn't look like that if he was waiting for her to say yes.

Heat spiraled through her, from the pit of her belly into her breasts and her face. What in hell was she thinking? She wouldn't. In fact, she should have slapped his face at his words. The sheikh wanted a new sexual toy and he figured she'd be thrilled to discover she was it.

He wasn't only crazy; he was insulting. She told him so, succinctly, coldly, carefully. And the SOB just smiled.

"I should have kept count of the number of times you've called me crazy tonight."

"Yes, you should. It might tell you something about your behavior, Lord Rashid."

"It's a little late for formality."

"It's never too late for formality and it's certainly not too late for sanity. Did you really think I'd agree to your offer?"

"Actually," he said, his mouth twitching just a little, "I thought you might slug me."

"An excellent idea." She stepped back, her hands on her hips, a look of contempt on her face. "I suppose it's been your experience that women become delirious with joy when you offer them such a wonderful opportunity."

Nick tucked his hands into his pockets. "I don't know. I've never, ah, made the offer before."

"Uh-huh. I'll just bet. Nicholas al Rashid, Lion of the Desert, Heir to the Imperial Throne, Lord of the Realm...and Celibate of the Century." She lifted a hand, examined her fingernails with care before looking at him again and flashing a toothy smile. "You never asked a woman to be your mistress?"

"No." He leaned back against the edge of the desk, crossed his feet at the ankles. "Usually the relationship simply...develops."

"Ah. You usually show a bit more finesse." She smiled brightly. "How nice."

Clearly, her sarcasm didn't impress him. He shrugged, his expression unchanging.

"Our situation is different. It called for a bolder move." His eyes, silver as rain, met hers. "You want a commission." The quiet tone in his voice changed just a little, took on a husky edge. "I want you."

Say something, Amanda told herself. Tell him he's being offensive, that he can't go around saying things like this to women. But he wasn't saying it to "women," he was saying it to her. She was the one he wanted. And she, heaven help her, and she...

Stop it!

She stood up straighter, cocked her chin and flashed a cool smile. "I see. You get a night in the sack. I get a job."

"No."

"Don't 'no' me, Lord Rashid." Amanda's tone hardened. "That's what you said. I'll sleep with you, and you'll give me a job. Do you have any idea how incredibly insulting and sleazy that offer is?"

Nick sighed and shook his head. "You're never going to make a success of—what was it? Benning Designs?"

"You're wrong. I'll make a huge success of it and I'll do it without accepting your charming proposition," she said caustically, "because I'm good. Damn good."

"You won't succeed," he said calmly, "unless you learn to pay attention." He folded his arms, lowered his chin, looked at her as if she'd just flunked the final exam in her business administration course. "I didn't say I wanted to sleep with you. I said I wanted you to be my mistress."

"It's the same thing."

"Not at all." Nick smiled coolly. "Sleeping with you would mean an hour of pleasure. Taking you as my mistress means pleasure for as long as our desire for each other lasts."

Heat seeped into her blood again, warmed her flesh and turned her bones to jelly. How could he talk so calmly about such a thing? Odder still, how could she hear those calm words and feel as if he were touching her skin?

"Either way, I'm not going to do it. I'd never trade my body for your checkbook."

"And a lovely body it is," Nick said, and uncoiled from the edge of the desk.

Amanda took a quick step back. The warning was there, burning in his eyes. "Nick," she said, "wait a minute—"

Her shoulders hit the wall as he moved forward. And when he reached for her, her heart leaped like a rabbit.

"I'll fight you," she said in a breathless whisper. "Nick, I swear..."

His hands encircled her wrists. That was all. He didn't kiss her, didn't gather her to him. Just that, the feel of his fingers on the pulse points in her wrists, but it was enough to turn her body liquid with desire.

"A spectacular body," he said softly. "And a face more beautiful than any I've ever seen." Nick lowered his head. She lifted hers. Lightly, lightly, he brushed his mouth across her slightly parted lips. "But I'm not asking for either in trade."

"No?" Amanda cleared her throat. Her voice sounded small and choked. "Then—then what's this all about?"

His eyes fell to her lips, then returned to lock with hers. "It's about desire," he murmured, and he bent his head and nuzzled the hair back from her face, pressed his hot mouth against her throat.

Don't, she thought, oh, don't. Don't fight. Don't move. Don't respond to him at all. But she trembled and made a little sound she couldn't prevent, and she knew that her pulse leaped under the stroke of his fingers.

"We're both intelligent adults, Amanda."

"Exactly. That's why I expect you to understand that what you want is impossible."

He smiled. "Anything is possible when you really want it."

She gave a little laugh that sounded forced even to her own ears, but it was the best she could manage at the moment. "Do you think I'm stupid? Or is that the plan, Nick? You're going to convince me of how foolish I am unless I agree to sleep..." She took a breath. Why was she arguing with him? He wanted something. She didn't. That was that. "Let go of me," she said.

He did. It was what she'd wanted, but she felt chilled without his hands on her, and that was silly. The night was warm. So was the room. And yet, without Nick to hold her...

Amanda swallowed, turned her back and walked to the window. It was very late. The moon had gone down and a breeze sighed around the windows. It made the shrubs that lined the terrace tremble under its touch, just as she had trembled under Nick's.

"You're right," she said, her voice low. "We're both adults. I'm not going to be coy and pretend I don't know what happens when you touch me. But I don't intend to give in to it." She took a breath, slowly let it out. "What went on in your bedroom? That wasn't me. You probably won't believe it, but I've never...I mean, no one has ever—"

"Except for me."

He spoke from just behind her, so close that all she had to do was take a step back to be in his arms again.

"Yes." She felt his hand move lightly over her hair and she fought back the urge to shut her eyes and give herself up to the caress. "But it won't happen again."

"I regret what happened, too." His voice thickened and he cleared his throat. "I've never come on to a woman with so little tact. I know I should apologize, but—"

"Don't." She spun around, looked at him, her cheeks on fire, her eyes glittering. "You wanted honesty. Well, the truth is that we were both at fault."

"We wanted each other. There's no fault in that."

"I don't much care how you choose to explain it, Nick. It was wrong. And I'm not going to change my mind about sleeping with—"

She gasped as he pulled her to him. "I could take you to bed right now."

"You could." Her chin rose and her eyes locked with his. "You're much stronger than I am."

His eyes went flat and cold. "Do you think I'm the kind of man who takes a woman by force?"

She didn't. She couldn't imagine him forcing himself on a woman any more than she could imagine a woman walking away from his bed.

"No," she whispered. "You're right. You wouldn't do that."

He shifted his weight, slid his hands up her body, leaving a trail of heat in the wake of his palms.

"All I'd have to do is kiss you. Touch you. How long would it take before you'd be naked in my arms, begging me to finish what we began in my bedroom hours ago?"

"No," she said again, but her voice trembled, and she couldn't meet his eyes.

"Yes," he said. "But that's not what I want. I want more. Much more."

He dropped his hands to his sides, turned away and walked across the small room. He stood with his back to Amanda, his hands clenched in his pockets.

Earlier tonight, in his bedroom, he'd wanted nothing more than a quick, hard ride. The blonde with the golden eyes beneath him, her skin slick with heat, her head thrown back...

That would have been enough.

Later, watching her drift from group to group at the party, seeing her make the best of what he knew had to be a difficult situation, he'd smiled a little, decided it might be pleasant to spend not an hour but a night with Amanda Benning in his bed.

Deanna had caught him looking. She'd said something cutting that was meant to remind him that his loyalty was supposed to be to her, but all she'd done was make him face what he'd known, and not admitted, for weeks.

He'd had enough of Deanna.

She was beautiful, but she was proof of the old adage. Beauty was, after all, only skin-deep. And so he'd taken her aside, gently told her that they were finished, and after a scene that had been uglier than he'd expected, he'd come back into the living room, taken one look at Amanda and realized she was drunk.

"Shall I deal with the lady, Lord Rashid?" Abdul had whispe ed, and Nick had sighed and said no, he'd take care of it...but somewhere between the living room and his study, he'd realized that he was wrong.

One night with Amanda wouldn't be enough.

He was hungry for her, and she was hungry for him, and only a fool would have imagined they'd have enough of each other between sunset and sunrise.

No, Nick thought, watching her face, one night wouldn't be sufficient. He wanted time to learn all the textures and tastes of this woman's mouth. Of the secret places of her body. She was a feast that would keep a man busy for a month of nights.

He turned and looked at her. "Have you ever gambled, Amanda?"

The sudden shift in conversation made her blink. "Gambled?"

"Yes. Did you ever bet on something?"

"No. Well, yes. I went to Las Vegas once. With my sisters. Sam played the slots. Carin played poker. I watched a roulette wheel for a while." Her brow furrowed. "What's this have to do with anything?"

"Indulge me," Nick said with a smile. He sat on the edge of the desk. "Did you bet? On the wheel, I mean?"

"Eventually."

"And?"

"And," she said, her chin lifting, daring him to say anything judgmental, "after I'd lost a hundred bucks, I quit."

Nick lifted his brows. "Interesting."

"I couldn't see the sense in losing more money."

"Ah. And you figured why bother betting unless you had a better chance of winning."

"Something like that."

"Suppose somebody offered you the chance to make a bet where you controlled the odds."

Something had changed in his smile. It made her uncomfortable. This whole conversation made her uncomfortable. She knew it was ridiculous, but talking about his wanting to sleep with her made her less uneasy than talking about bets and stakes and odds.

"Well," she said, "that, um, that would be, um, interesting."

Not as interesting as the way he was looking at her. His gaze was intense, as if she were the only thing in the universe worthy of his attention. It was flattering. It was disturbing. It reminded her of something she'd almost forgotten.

Once, just after her mother had married Jonas and gone to live at Espada, she'd visited the ranch and gone horseback riding in the hills that surrounded it. She'd dismounted beside a clear-running stream, tied the reins to a tree branch, strolled maybe a hundred yards—and come almost face-to-face with a cougar.

The cat had looked at her. She'd looked at the cat. And when it finally hissed and melted into the trees, she'd known that she'd gotten away because it had chosen to let her go, not because she'd been brave enough to stare it down.

That was how she felt now. Her heart gave a little shiver. As if she'd gone for an innocent stroll and ended up face-to-face with a cougar.

Nick reached back, slid open a drawer in the desk, took something from it. A coin, she saw. A bright silver coin. He smiled, tossed it, caught it in his hand. "Heads or tails," he said. "What do you think?"

"I think it's time I went home. Good night, Nick. It's certainly been—"

"Scared?"

She sighed, rolled her eyes, folded her arms over her chest. "Heads."

"Heads it is." The coin spun through the air. Nick caught it, showed it to her. "Good guess. How about another try?"

"Oh, for heaven's... Heads."

He tossed the coin again, caught it, held out his hand. The silver piece lay, heads up, in his palm.

"Great," she said with an artificial smile.

"One last time." Nick tossed the coin. It spun like quicksilver before he caught it and closed his fingers around it. "What's it going to be this time? Heads or tails?"

"This is… Okay, I'll humor you. Tails. It has to be. I remember enough of my college stats course to know that the odds of it coming up heads again are…"

He opened his hand. She blinked.

"…One in six," she said, and frowned. "How'd you do that?"

He smiled, tossed the coin to her. She caught it, examined it, then looked at him.

"Heads on both sides," she said. "It's a phony."

"The gentleman who gave it to me preferred to refer to it as a device for assuring a positive outcome."

Nick grinned. She almost smiled back at him. He had, she thought, a wonderful smile…but then she thought of the cougar, of how she could never have matched either its strength or its cunning, and she felt more like running than smiling.

"If there's a point here," she said carefully, "I don't get it."

He rose to his feet, came slowly toward her, his smile gone. The room seemed to have reduced in size until there was barely space in it for the both of them. Foolishly, she held out the coin. Nick shook his head, took her hand, folded her fingers around it.

"Keep it," he said softly.

"I—I don't want it. I don't—"

"Amanda." He clasped her shoulders, slid his hands down her arms, twined his fingers with hers. "We're going to make a bet, you and I." A slow, sexy smile curled across his mouth. "A bet that will assure you of a positive outcome."

"Nick, I told you. I don't gamble. Just that one time…"

"You're going to give me a week of your life."

Her eyes widened. "A week of my—"

"One week." He kissed her, his mouth tender, soft against hers. "Just seven days."

"Nick, listen to me. You can't just—"

"When the week ends, I'll sign a contract with Benning Designs."

"Damn you!" Amanda jerked her hands free. "Haven't you heard a word I said? I won't sleep with you for a contract."

"No," he said softly, "I'm sure you won't."

"Great. We understand each other. Now, I'm going to open this door. And you're not going to stop me."

"I'll sign the contract whether you've slept with me or not."

"What?" She moved past him, dragged a hand through her hair. "What is this? Another quaint custom straight from the homeland? I wasn't born yesterday. Do you really think I believe life is like that coin of yours? Heads on both sides?" She frowned, opened her hand and looked at the quarter. "Where'd you get this anyway?"

Nick sighed. "It's a long, dull story."

"Amazing." She smiled brightly. "I just happen to be in the mood for a long, dull story."

"I was sixteen, and I stopped to watch a guy working a three-card-monte game in Greenwich Village. Each time he thought a mark—"

"A what?"

"A player." Nick grinned. "Or, more accurately, a loser. Whenever he thought a loser was going to leave, he'd take a coin from his pocket, show it and say, 'Call it. Double or nothing.' It never came up anything but heads."

"And the reason the Heir to the Imperial Throne was standing on a corner, betting against a street hustler, was…?"

"Well, it was fun."

"Fun," she said dryly.

"Yeah. I was at a private prep school."

"Of course," Amanda said politely.

"My tuition was paid, but my father was strict about my allowance. I wanted more money for something—I don't recall what. And my mother was in Europe, making a movie.

Anyway, I was pretty good with cards. It was a weekend and I had nothing better to do—''

"So you went down to the village and got hustled." She narrowed her eyes at him. He had to have invented the story. The Lion of the Desert, a cardsharp? "And, what? The guy gave you the coin?"

He laughed softly. "I paid him twenty bucks for it. I figured it made a great souvenir."

"Uh-huh. He hustled you. And now you're trying to hustle me. Did you really think I'd fall for that?" Amanda tossed the coin on the desk. "The 'you give me a week and I'll give you a contract' routine?"

"Well, no." Nick put one hand on the wall beside her and slid the other around the back of her head. "Actually, I didn't."

"Ha," she said, and tried to pretend she didn't feel the drift of his fingers along the nape of her neck. "I knew there was a catch."

He gave her the kind of smile that made her heart try to wedge its way into her throat. "I meant what I said. You'll give me a week. If we become lovers, you get the contract. If we don't..." He took her hand and brought it to his mouth. "If we don't, you still get the contract." His eyes met hers, and what she saw in them made her feel dizzy. "But if you do give yourself to me," he said softly, "then you'll agree to be my mistress. To be available only to me, accessible only to me, for as long as it suits us both." A quick smile angled across his mouth. "Despite what you may think, I believe in equality of the sexes."

His words, the way he was looking at her, conjured up images more erotic than anything she'd ever experienced in a man's arm. Talk, that was all it was. Not even Nicholas al Rashid could really expect her to accept such a proposition.

"I mean every word," he said softly.

She tilted her head up, stared into his eyes and knew, with breathtaking certainty, that he did.

He turned her hand over, brought it to his mouth again, kissed the soft flesh at the base of her thumb. "Are you afraid to trust yourself?"

Amanda laughed. "Such modesty. Do you really think—"

He kissed her even though he knew it was a mistake. The last thing a wise man would do right now was give Amanda Benning graphic proof of how sure he was he'd win the bet.

But he'd underestimated her. She made a little sound as their mouths met, but that soft, sweet whisper of breath was the only sign she gave of the emotional storm he knew raged within her. It made what lay ahead all the more exciting.

"You're very sure of yourself, Lord Rashid."

"As are you, Ms. Benning." He smiled. "You'll be a worthy adversary."

"*If* I were to accept your proposition. But it's out of the question. It's so outlandish."

"Is it?"

She started to answer, caught herself just in time and wondered if this was really happening.

Yes. Yes, it was.

Twenty-five stories below, a siren wailed through the night. Music from the party drifted under the door. Life was going on all around them; people were doing the things people did on a warm evening in Manhattan...and she stood here, discussing whether or not she'd agree to become the mistress of a man she hardly knew.

It wouldn't happen. There wasn't even a remote possibility she'd let Nick seduce her. He was handsome. All right. He was gorgeous. He was rich and powerful and he ruled a desert kingdom.

But a man would need more than that to get her into his bed. She was a twenty-first-century American woman. She was educated and independent and she couldn't be lured into a man's arms like some trembling virgin.

What she *could* do was win the bet.

A week. That was all he'd asked. Seven days of what would

basically be simple dating. And, at the end of those days, she'd walk away from Nicholas al Rashid with her virtue intact, a contract in her pocket. She'd give the man who thought he could buy everything a lesson in how to choke down a large helping of humble pie.

She had to admit the possibility was intriguing.

"Well?" Nick said.

Amanda looked at him. She could read nothing in his face, not even desire. Oh, yes. He'd be very good, playing cards.

"Tell me," she said softly, "have you ever wanted something you couldn't have?"

"You're doing it again. Answering a question with a question."

"You've asked me to allow you to try to seduce me." She smiled tightly. "I think that entitles me to ask as many questions as I like."

"Are you afraid I'll succeed?"

"Seduction requires a seducer and a seducee, Lord Rashid. You can't succeed unless I cooperate." This time, her smile was dazzling. "And I promise you, I'd never do that."

"Is that a yes?"

Her eyes met his. She could see something there now, glinting in the silver depths. *What do you think you're doing, Amanda?* a voice inside her whispered.

"There'd have to be rules," she said.

"Name them."

"No force."

"I'm not a man who believes in forcing himself on a woman."

"No tricks."

"Certainly not."

"And I don't want anybody to know that we've entered into this—this wager." She hesitated. "It would be difficult to explain."

"Done."

He held out his hand as if they were concluding a business

deal. She looked at it, then at him. *Amanda,* the voice said desperately, *Amanda…*

She took a quick step back. "I'll—I'll think about it," she said, the words coming out in a rush.

Nick reached for her. "You already did."

And then his mouth was on hers, she was curling her arms tightly around his neck, and the wager was on.

CHAPTER SEVEN

AT FOUR forty-three in the morning, Nicholas al Rashid, Lion of the Desert, Lord of the Realm and Sublime Heir to the Imperial Throne of Quidar, gave up all attempts at sleep. He threw back the blankets, swung his legs to the floor, ran his fingers through his tousled hair and tried to decide exactly when he'd lost his mind.

A man had to be crazy to do the things he'd done tonight. He'd found a woman going through his things, accused her of spying, made passionate love to her, locked her in his closet and, in a final show of lunacy, fast-talked her into a wager so weird he still couldn't believe he'd come up with it.

"Hell," Nick muttered.

He rose, paced back and forth enough times to wear a path in the silk carpet, pulled on a pair of jeans and went quietly down the stairs.

Not quietly enough, though. He'd hardly entered the kitchen when a light came on in the hallway that led to Abdul's rooms. A moment later, the old man stood in the doorway, wearing a robe and blinking against the light.

"Excellency?"

It was, Nick thought with mild surprise, the first time he'd ever seen Abdul wearing anything but a black, somewhat shiny, suit.

"Yes, Abdul. It's me."

"Is something wrong, sire?"

"No, nothing. I just… Go on back to bed, Abdul."

"Did you want a sandwich?"

"Thank you, no."

"Some tea? Coffee? I shall wake the cook."

94

"No!" Nick took a breath and forced a smile to his lips. "I don't need the cook, Abdul. I just—I'm thirsty, that's all."

"Of course, sire." Abdul bustled into the kitchen. "What would you like? Mineral water? Spirits? Sherry? You're right, there's no need to wake the cook. I'll—"

"Abdul," Nick said pleasantly but firmly, "go back to bed."

"But, my lord—"

"Good night, Abdul."

The little man hesitated. Nick could see that he wanted to say something more, but custom prevented it. And a good thing, too, he thought grimly, because he had the feeling his secretary had developed as many doubts about his sanity as he had.

"Very well, Lord Rashid. If you change your mind—"

"I'll call you."

Abdul nodded, bowed and backed out of the room. Nick waited until the hall light went out. Then he opened the refrigerator, peered inside, found a bottle of the New England ale he'd developed a taste for back in his university days, and popped the cap. Bottle in hand, he walked through the darkened apartment and out onto the terrace.

The city lay silent below him.

At this hour on a Sunday morning, traffic was sparse, the sound of it muted. Central Park stretched ahead of him, its green darkness broken by the diamond glow of lamps that marked its paths.

Nick leaned against the low wall, tilted the bottle of ale to his lips, took a long drink and wished he were home. There'd been times before when he'd felt like this, when thoughts had whirled through his head and sleep had refused to come. The night before he'd left for Yale and a course of study that he knew would set him irrevocably on the path toward eventual leadership of his people. The night word had come of his mother's death in a plane crash. The night before he'd left for New York and the responsibilities that came with representing his country's financial affairs...

Nick took another drink.

Each time, he'd found peace by riding his Arabian stallion into the desert, alone under the night sky, the moon and the majestic light of the stars.

He sighed, turned his back to the city and swallowed another mouthful of ale. There was no desert to give him solace now. He was trapped in the whirlwind of his thoughts and the knowledge that nothing he'd done tonight made sense.

He wasn't a man who'd ever forced himself on a woman, yet he'd come close to doing that with Amanda Benning. Not that he'd have needed force. The way she'd melted against him. The way she'd returned his kisses, fitted her body to his...

Nick held the bottle of ale against his forehead, rolled it back and forth to cool his skin.

And that proposal he'd made her. Give me a week, he'd said. If I can seduce you, you'll agree to be my mistress.

Talk about acting like a second-rate Valentino, he thought, and groaned again. It was ludicrous. Besides, who knew if he'd even want her more than once? The lady might turn out to be a dud in bed instead of a smoldering ember just waiting to be fanned into an inferno.

"Dammit!"

Nick swung around and glared out over the quiet park. What was wrong with him? He was standing alone in the middle of the night, thinking about a woman he hardly knew, and doing one fine job of turning himself on.

Okay, so she'd probably be good in bed. Terrific, even. There really wasn't much doubt about that. Still, a man needed more than sex from a mistress. Well, he did anyway. She had to be interesting and have a sense of humor. She had to like some of the things he liked. Riding, for instance. Walking in the rain. Could she watch the film, *When Harry Met Sally,* for the third or fourth time and still laugh over that scene in the delicatessen?

Nick frowned. What was he thinking? So what if it turned out Amanda didn't like those things? Deanna certainly didn't.

Rain made her hair frizzy, she said. Movies were boring the second time around. And riding was best done in a limousine, not on a horse.

The women who'd come before her had tastes different from his, too.

All he'd ever asked of a woman was that she be attractive, fun and, of course, good in bed. If Amanda had those qualifications, fine. He wanted to sleep with her, not live with her. And she'd agreed.

He was making a mountain out of a molehill. It was a bet, that was all it was. And he'd win it. He had no doubt about that. They'd go to bed together and he'd take it from there.

The sky was lightening, changing from the black of night to the pink of dawn. Somewhere in the leafy bowers of the park, a bird chirped a sleepy homage to that first hint of day.

Nick yawned and stretched, then decided he felt much better. Amazing what a little clear thinking could do. Okay, then. In a while, he'd tell Abdul to call Amanda and inform her that his car would pick her up at, say, seven this evening. That would get her here by seven-thirty for drinks and dinner.

If they ever made it to dinner, he thought with a little smile. As wagers went, this was the best he'd ever made. How come he'd wasted half the night figuring that out?

He strolled back through the darkened penthouse, put the empty bottle neatly on the kitchen counter, went up to his bedroom, pulled off his jeans and threw himself across the bed on his belly. He closed his eyes, yawned, punched his pillow into shape...

Twenty minutes later, he was still awake, lying on his back with his hands clasped under his head as he stared up at the ceiling. The distant whisper of the fax machine came as a relief.

Nick put on his jeans and went down to his study. The fax was long and still coming in. He plucked the first page from the basket, smiled as he read his father's warm greeting, but his smile changed to a frown as he read further.

His father, whose Arabian horses were world renowned, had

reached agreement with an old American friend. He'd arranged to fly a stallion to the States in exchange for the friend's gift of a Thoroughbred mare. He hated to impose upon Nicholas on such short notice, etc. etc., but would he meet with the friend and work out the details in person?

Nick huffed out a breath. He would do it, of course. It would mean a day, perhaps two, spent out of the city, time during which he wouldn't be able to do what he had to do to win his wager with Amanda.

"Oh, for God's sake," Nick said, and tossed the fax on the table.

Enough was enough. The truth was, the bet was a bad one. A man didn't win a woman as if she were the stakes in a hand of poker. He didn't tempt her into his arms with a contract.

A smart man wouldn't want Amanda Benning at all. She was as prickly as a porcupine, as unpredictable as the weather. She was city heat; she was desert night. She was either the roommate who'd pointed his sister toward trouble seven years ago or the one who'd been wise enough to avoid it.

The one, the only, thing she absolutely was, was female.

So what?

He'd wearied of Deanna. That had to be the reason he'd been attracted to Amanda. Right?

"Right," Nick muttered.

Well, he could be attracted to another woman just as easily. He could have any woman he wanted. He could have his choice—blondes, brunettes and redheads in such profusion they'd cause a traffic jam, just lining up outside the door.

Nick went back upstairs, pulled on a white T-shirt and tucked it into his jeans. He put on sneakers, grabbed his wallet, his keys and his cell phone, went down the steps and into his private elevator. There was only one way to deal with this. He'd go to see Amanda, tell her the bet was off and put this whole foolish episode behind him.

He was in the elevator, halfway to the underground garage, when he realized he didn't have the slightest idea where she lived.

"Hell," he said wearily, punched the button for the penthouse and headed back the way he'd come. Was she in the phone book? he wondered as the door slid open...but he didn't have to bother checking. There, lying forlornly on a table, was one of those little business cards she'd been handing out like souvenirs.

Nick picked it up, lifted it to his nostrils. The card still bore a trace of her perfume. He shut his eyes, saw her as she'd gone from guest to guest, chin up, back straight, facing down the whispers and making the best of a difficult situation.

He frowned, looked at the address, then tucked the card into his pocket and rode the elevator down again. If the situation had been tough, it was her fault, not his. The only thing he cared about now was making sure she understood that he wasn't the least bit interested in following through on their bet.

Not in the slightest, he thought as his Ferrari shot like a missile into the quiet of the Sunday morning streets.

Amanda sat cross-legged in the center of her bed and watched the hands of the clock creep from 6:05 to 6:06.

Was the clock broken? She reached for it, held it to her ear. *Ticktock,* it said, *ticktock,* which was what it had been saying since she'd checked it the first time, somewhere around four.

She frowned, set the clock down on the night table and wrapped her arms around her knees. The only thing that wasn't working was her common sense.

What on earth had she done?

"You said you'd sleep with Nicholas al Rashid," she muttered. "*That's* what you've done."

No. Her frown deepened as she unfolded her legs and got out of bed. No, she thought coldly, she most definitely had not done anything as simple as that.

What she'd done was agree to become Nick's newest sexual toy, assuming he managed to seduce her in the next seven days.

God, it was hot in here!

She padded to the window where an ancient air conditioner wheezed like the Boston terrier her mother had once owned. She put her hand to the vents and waggled her fingers. An anemic flow of cool air sighed over her skin.

"Great," she said. No wonder she couldn't sleep.

Amanda jerked her nightgown over her head, marched into the bathroom and stepped into the shower, gasping at the shock of the cold water. It was the only way to stay cool in this tiny oven of an apartment. The place was so hot that when she'd awakened at four, she'd been drenched in very unlady-like sweat.

She lowered her head and let the water beat against the nape of her neck,

She'd been dreaming just before she awoke. A silly dream, something straight out of a silent movie. Nick had been dressed in a flowing white robe and riding a white horse. She'd been seated behind him, her arms tight around his waist, her cheek pressed to his back. And then the scene had shifted, and he'd been carrying her into a tent hung with royal-blue silk.

"Amanda," he'd said softly as he lowered her to her feet, and she'd sighed and lifted her mouth for his kiss....

Shower or no shower, she was hot again. But not from the dream. Certainly not from the dream. It was the apartment, she thought briskly. The stuffy, awful apartment.

Amanda turned off the water and blotted herself dry. She ran her fingers through her hair, tugged an oversized cotton T-shirt and cotton bikini panties over her still-damp skin and headed for the kitchen.

"Forget about sleep," she muttered.

Obviously, it wasn't a very good idea to drink lots of champagne before bedtime, especially if you spent the time between the wine and the attempt at sleep in the arms of a man who thought he could talk you into something he was certain you couldn't possibly refuse.

She filled the kettle with water, set it on the stove and turned on the burner.

Thought, Amanda?

"Let's be honest here," she said.

Nick *had* talked her into it. And—to stay with the honesty thing—he hadn't had to work all that hard to do it.

What a smooth character he was. Proposing a wager like that, making it sound so simple...

But, of course, it was.

Amanda sighed, walked to the window and gazed at the view. It wasn't exactly Central Park, but she could see a tree. All she had to do was stand on her toes, crook her neck, tilt her head and aim at a spot beyond the fire escape.

Nick wouldn't know what that was like. To have to contort yourself for a view. For anything. What Lord Rashid wanted, Lord Rashid got.

And Lord Rashid wanted her.

Well, he wasn't going to have her. And wouldn't that come as a huge surprise? All he'd get out of their wager was a handsomely furnished home. As for a woman to warm his bed—he'd always have plenty of those. A man like that would.

The kettle whistled. She turned off the stove, took a mug from the cupboard, dumped a tea bag into it and then filled it with water. She looked at the sugar bowl, turned away, then looked at it again.

"The hell with it," she said, and reached for the bowl.

Calories didn't count tonight. Comfort did, and if that meant two, well, three heaping spoonfuls of that bad-for-you, terrible-for-your-teeth and worse-for-your-waistline overprocessed white stuff, so be it.

"Ah," she said after her first sip.

The tea tasted wonderful. Funny how a hot liquid could make you feel cooler. She hadn't believed it until she'd spent a couple of weeks visiting her mother in Texas last year.

"Hot tea cools you off," Marta had insisted, and when Amanda finally tried it and agreed it was true, she'd hugged her and smiled. "You just come to me for advice, sweetie, and I'll always steer you right."

Amanda took another sip of tea as she walked through her

postage-stamp living room, sank into a rocker she'd rescued from a sidewalk where it had awaited death in the jaws of a garbage truck, and watched the sun claw its way up the brick sides of the city.

What advice would her mother offer about Nick? That was easy. She knew exactly what Marta would say.

"Mandy, you have to telephone that man this minute and tell him you can't possibly agree to the wager. A lady does not bet her virtue."

Excellent advice it would be, too.

Not that she was afraid she'd lose the bet. Amanda took a drink of tea and leaned back in the rocker. A woman who didn't want to be seduced couldn't be seduced. It was just that the implications of the wager were—well, they were...

Sleazy? Immoral?

"Humiliating," she mumbled.

Yes, she would call Nick and tell him the wager was off. She'd reached that conclusion hours ago. How best to do it, though? That was the problem.

She'd thought about calling Dawn for suggestions, but then she'd have to tell her all the details, and what, exactly, was there to say?

Hi, sorry we didn't get the chance to spend any time together last night. Are you okay? And oh, by the way, I've agreed to become your brother's mistress if he can first lure me into his bed.

No way. Discussing this with Dawn wasn't even an option. Neither was discussing it with Marta. How could a daughter tell her mother she'd even considered a proposal like that?

Amanda drank some more tea.

She could call one of her sisters for help, but there wasn't much sense in that, either. Carin would just tell her, in that irritatingly proper tone of voice, that if a deal sounded too good to be true, it probably was. As for Samantha...she couldn't begin to imagine what Sam would say unless it was something outrageously facetious, maybe that the deal sounded like lots of fun if it weren't for all the bother involved.

"Fun," Amanda muttered, and drained the last sugary drops from the mug.

Okay, then. She'd just have to do the deed without consulting anybody but herself. Phone Nick, tell him she was sorry but she'd changed her mind. Not that she was afraid she'd lose their bet, but...

Amanda scowled. Why did she keep telling herself that? Certainly she wouldn't lose it.

Someday she'd tell her sisters the story. They'd laugh and laugh; the whole thing would be one big joke.

"He was a sheikh," she'd say, "and he said, 'Come wiz me to zee Casbah.'"

Except he hadn't. If only he had. If he'd played the scene as if he'd stolen it from a bad movie, with a smoldering look and a twirl of his mustache...

She groaned and closed her eyes.

The truth was, Nick was gorgeous and sexy. He could have any woman he wanted, but he wanted her.

She had to admit it was thrilling. Maybe that was the reason she'd lost all perspective. Maybe it was why she'd let him fast-talk her into agreeing to a bet on her own morality.

Was that the doorbell? Amanda sat up straight. Who'd be at her door at this hour? This building had awful security, but still, did burglars really ring the bell and announce themselves?

The bell rang again. She rose to her feet and hurried to the door. "Who is it?"

"It's Nick."

Nick? Her heart thumped. She opened the peephole, peered out. It *was* Nick, and he didn't look happy.

"Nick." Her mouth felt as dry as cotton. "Nick, you should have called first. I—"

"I didn't want to wake you."

"You didn't want to wake me? What did you think leaning on my doorbell at—at what, six in the morning, would do?"

"It's seven-thirty, and if you want to have a discussion about the propriety of phoning first, I'd prefer having it in your apartment. Open the door, please, Amanda."

Open the door. Admit Nick into this tiny space. Into *her* space, where he'd seem twice as tall, twice as big, twice as commanding.

"Amanda." There was no "please" this time. She jumped as his fist thudded against the door. "Open up!"

She heard a lock click, a door creak open. Oh, God. Her neighbors were preparing themselves for a bit of street theater. New Yorkers might live on the same floor in an apartment building, collect their mail at lobby boxes ranged side by side and never so much as make eye contact, but she suspected none of them would pass up a little drama going on right in the hall.

Amanda rose on the balls of her bare feet, put her eye to the peephole and looked at Nick. "People are listening," she whispered.

"And watching," he said coldly. "Perhaps you'd like to sell tickets."

She stepped back, slipped the lock, the chain and the night bolt. The door swung open and he stepped inside.

"An excellent decision," he said, and shut the door behind him.

"What are you doing here, Nick?"

What was he doing there? Just for a second, he couldn't quite remember. Amanda was standing before him, barefooted. She was wearing a loose T-shirt and nothing else. Nothing he could see anyway. Her hair was tousled, her face was scrubbed and shiny, and he couldn't imagine anything more urgent than finding out if she tasted as sweet and fresh as she looked.

But that wasn't why he'd come here, Nick reminded himself, and folded his arms. "I want to talk," he said.

"Good." She lifted her chin. "That's—that's really good. Because I—I..." She stopped, the words catching in her throat, and stared at him.

"What's the matter?"

"You're not wearing a tux."

"No." His smile was all teeth. "No, actually, I've been known to get through an entire day without feeling the need to put on a pair of pants with satin stripes down the legs."

"I didn't mean—it's just that you look—you remind me—"

"Of the night we first met." She was right, he thought, and gave her a long, measuring look, except she was older now, and the soft curves outlined beneath the cotton shirt were more lush. "Instant replay," he said, and flashed a smile that upped the temperature in the room another ten degrees.

Amanda stepped back. "I'm not dressed," she said, and blushed when she realized how stupid she sounded. "For company. If you'll just wait—"

"I've been awake half the night. I'll be damned if I'll wait any longer."

"Look, Nick, I want to talk, too. About that bet. Just let me put on some clothes."

"You're already wearing clothes." His voice turned husky as he took a step toward her. "What else would you call what you have on?"

Provocative, he thought, silently answering his own question, although how a T-shirt could be provocative was beyond him to comprehend. He liked his women in silk. In lace. In things that flowed and shimmered.

"Nick?"

"Yes." Somehow, he was standing a breath away from her. Somehow, his hands were on her hips. Somehow, he was bunching the cotton fabric in his hands, lifting it, sliding it up her skin and revealing the smallest pair of white cotton panties he'd ever seen.

"Nick." Her voice was barely a whisper. Her head was tilted back; her eyes were huge, luminous and locked with his. "Nick, the bet is—"

He bent his head, brushed his mouth over hers. She gave a delicate moan, and he cupped her breasts, felt the delicate weight and silken texture of them in his palms. He feathered his thumbs over the crests and Amanda moaned again, trembled against him and lifted herself to his hungry embrace.

He kissed her over and over, offered her the intimacy of his tongue, groaned when she touched it with her own, then sucked it into the heat of her mouth. He backed her against the wall; she gave a cry of protest as he took his lips from hers to peel off her shirt, then his.

Oh, the feel of her satin skin against his, when he took her back into his arms. The softness of her breasts against the hardness of his chest. He trembled, felt the air driven from his lungs.

"Amanda," he whispered, and she sighed and kissed him, breathed a soft "yes" against his lips as he lifted her off her feet and into his arms—

A buzz sounded from his pocket.

"Nick?"

His pocket buzzed again.

"Nick." Amanda tore her mouth from his. "Something's buzzing."

He lifted his head, his breathing harsh. She was right. His cell phone was making sounds like an angry wasp. He mouthed an oath, let her down to her feet, kept an arm firmly around her as he dug the phone from his jeans.

"What?" he snarled.

"Sire."

Nick's eyes narrowed. "Abdul. This had better be important."

"It is, my lord. There is a fax from your father. I thought you would wish to know of it."

The color was high in Amanda's cheeks. He could read her eyes, see her growing embarrassment. She looked up at him, shook her head and tried to step away. Nick bent quickly and kissed her, his mouth soft against hers until, at last, she kissed him back.

"Lord Rashid? There is a fax—"

"I already saw it, Abdul. Goodbye."

"Excellency, it is a second fax and arrived only moments

ago. Your father asks if you would fly to this place called Texas—''

"He asked me that in the first fax. Dammit, Abdul—''

"He asks if you would fly there today. The stallion he sent arrived much sooner than expected, and the animal has been hurt in transit.''

Nick uttered a violent oath. The only place he wanted to be right now was in Amanda's bedroom, but he knew the importance of duty and obligation. Would the woman in his arms be as understanding?

"Call the pilot,'' he said gruffly. "Have him ready the plane. You are to pack me some clothes, Abdul. Meet me at the hangar in an hour with the things I'll need.''

Abdul was still speaking when Nick hit the disconnect button, tossed the phone aside and tried to gather Amanda close to him again, but she was unyielding, moving only her arms, crossing them over her naked breasts in a classic feminine gesture that somehow went straight to his heart.

"It's good that you're leaving.'' Her voice was steady, but her face was pale. "You're not to come here again, Lord Rashid. I know I agreed to the terms of our wager, but—''

"The wager is off, Amanda. I came here to tell you that.'' Her golden eyes widened; he knew it wasn't what she'd expected him to say. He wanted to draw her close and kiss her until the color returned to her cheeks. Instead, he picked up her discarded shirt and wrapped it gently around her. "Here,'' he said softly. "You must be cold.''

Cold? She was swimming in heat from his touch, from imagining what would have happened if Abdul hadn't called—but she knew better than to let him know that.

"Thank you,'' she said stiffly.

"I don't want you as my mistress because of a bet,'' Nick said, his eyes locked to hers. "I want you to be mine because you desire no other man but me. Because you find joy only in my arms.''

Her heartbeat stumbled, but the look she gave him was sharp and clear.

"You amaze me," she said with a polite smile. "You're always so sure you'll get what you want."

"We'd be making love right now if that call hadn't interrupted us."

"I'm not going to argue with you."

"No." He smiled. "You won't, because there's nothing to argue about. You know that I'm right."

She took a step back. "I want you to leave. Right now."

"I don't think that's what you want at all."

He moved quickly, drew her into his arms and kissed her. She told herself his kisses meant nothing, that she wouldn't respond...but it was Nick who ended the kiss, not she.

"All right," she said stiffly, "you've proved your point. Yes, I—I've thought about what it would be like to—to..." She gave a shuddering breath. "But it would be wrong. I know that. And, unlike you, I don't always give in to my desires."

"Why would it be wrong?"

"Why?" Her laugh was forced and abrupt. "Well, because...because...dammit, I don't have to justify my decision to you!"

"You can't even justify it to yourself." Nick put his hand under her chin and tipped her head up until their eyes met. "I can't get out of this trip, Amanda. Do you understand?"

"I'm not a child," she said coldly. "Certainly I understand. You're going away on business and you'd like me to be waiting for you when you get back. Well, I'm sorry to disappoint you, Lord Rashid, but I won't be."

"You won't have to be, not if you go with me."

"What?"

"We'll only be gone a day or two." He bent his head, brushed his mouth over hers. "Come with me, Amanda."

"No!" She laughed again and tried to wrench free of his hands. "You must think I'm an idiot!"

"I think you're a woman with more courage than she gives herself credit for. And I think you want to say yes."

"Well, you think wrong. We've agreed our wager is—"

"Off. And it is." *And what, exactly, was he doing?* He

never mixed business with pleasure. Then again, this wasn't really a business trip. It was just a couple of days on a ranch in Texas. "Come with me," he urged, rushing the words together, knowing that his thinking was somehow flawed, that it would be dangerous to think too long or hard about what he was asking her to do. "We'll simply be a man and a woman, getting to know each other."

"I know you already. You're a man who can't take no for an answer. Besides, I can't just—just up and leave. I have a business to run."

"And I'm your client. Don't look so surprised, sweetheart. I said our wager was off. I didn't say I wanted to go on living in an apartment that looks like an expensive hotel suite." Nick linked his hands in the small of Amanda's back. "If you come with me, you can ask me all the questions you like. About my tastes. My preferences. You need to know them in order to decorate my home, don't you?"

"Yes." She chewed on her lip. "But..."

But what? He was making it sound as if going away with him was the most logical thing in the world, but it wasn't. She'd just trembled in his arms. His hands had been on her breasts, and oh, she'd wanted more. Much more. She'd wanted to touch him as he'd touched her. To lie naked in his arms, to feel the weight of him as he filled her—

"Amanda?"

His voice was low and rough. She didn't dare look at him because she knew what she'd see in his eyes.

"We'll talk. Only talk, if that's what you want." Nick raised her face to his. "Say you'll come with me."

She knew what her answer should be. But she gave him the answer they both wanted—with her kiss.

CHAPTER EIGHT

NICK wouldn't tell her where they were going.

"It's a surprise," he said, when she asked.

He knew it was crazy not to tell her, but what if he said they were flying to a ranch in Texas and she said she hated ranches and everything about them? What if she said she didn't like riding fast and hard across the open range? It might turn out she'd never seen a horse except maybe in Central Park and that would be all right just so long as she smiled and said yes, that would be wonderful, when he offered to teach her to ride.

"Hell," Nick muttered as he paced the length of Amanda's living room.

Maybe he really was crazy. He'd met this woman last night. Well, he'd met her years ago, but he'd never gotten to know her until last night, never held her in his arms until then. What did it matter if she liked horses or hated them? If she didn't want to sit behind him in the saddle, her arms wrapped around his waist, her breasts pressed to his back as they rode not across the green hills of north-central Texas but over the hot desert sands?

Crazy was the word, he thought grimly, and swung toward the closed bedroom door. All right. He'd knock on the door, tell her politely that he'd changed his mind. She was right. There was no reason for her to go with him. He'd phone when he got back and they'd have drinks, perhaps dinner....

The door opened just as he reached it. Amanda stood in the opening, holding a small carry-on bag. "I packed only what you said I'd need. Jeans. Shirts." She gave a little laugh. "I don't know why you're being so mysterious about this trip. I

110

mean, it's hard to know what to take when you don't know the destination. What is it, Nick?''

Her face was flushed, her eyes bright. She was wearing jeans and a cotton shirt, she hadn't bothered putting any makeup on her face, and he wanted to tell her he'd never seen a more beautiful woman in his life.

"Whatever you've packed is fine," he said gruffly, and he took the carry-on from her, linked his fingers through hers and tried to figure out exactly what was happening to him.

His plane was a small, sleek jet.

Amanda had flown in private aircraft before. Two of her stepbrothers owned their own planes. Her stepfather did, too; in fact, Jonas had a small jet, similar to Nick's in size—but Jonas's plane didn't have a fierce lion painted on the fuselage.

Nobody bowed to Jonas, either, but half a dozen people bowed as Nick approached the jet, half-prostrating themselves even though he waved them all quickly to their feet.

The Lion of the Desert, Amanda thought. Goose bumps rose on her skin. Yesterday, the words had been nothing but a title. A silly one, at that. Now, for the first time, she looked at the stern profile of the man walking beside her and realized that he was, in fact, a prince.

She tore her hand from his and stumbled to a halt.

"Amanda?"

"Nick." She spoke quickly, breathlessly. Her heart was racing as if she'd run here from her apartment instead of riding in Nick's Ferrari. "I can't go with you. I can't—"

Nick clasped her shoulders and turned her to face him. "My people won't blink an eye if I lift you into my arms and carry you on board," he said softly. "You could scream and kick, but they'd ignore you. Kidnapping a woman and keeping her in his harem is still the prerogative of the prince of the realm."

He was smiling. He was teasing her; she knew that. Still, she could imagine it happening. Nick, scooping her up in his arms. Carrying her onto the plane. Taking her high into the clouds, stripping away her defenses as he stripped away her clothes because yes, she wanted him. Wanted him...

"I made you a promise, sweetheart. And I'll keep it. You'll be safe. I won't touch you unless you want me to."

He held out his hand. She hesitated.

Have you ever gambled, Amanda?

The question, and her answer, were laughable. What was losing a hundred dollars at the roulette wheel compared to what she stood to lose now? And, thinking it, she put her hand in his.

He led her into a luxurious compartment done in deep shades of blue and gold. A pair of comfortable upholstered chairs flanked a small sofa. Everywhere she looked she saw the embroidered image of the same fierce lion that was painted on the outside of the plane.

"The Lion of the Desert," she said softly.

To her surprise, Nick blushed. "I suppose it seems melodramatic to someone who's lived only in the United States, but it's the seal of Quidar. It's been the emblem of my people for three thousand years."

"It's not melodramatic at all." Amanda looked at him. "It must be wonderful, being part of something so ancient and honorable."

"Yes," he said after a few seconds, "it is. Not everyone understands that. In this age of computers and satellites—"

"Of small, swift jets," she said with a little smile.

"Yes. In these times, it would be easy to forget the old ways. But they're important. They're to be honored even when it's difficult..." He paused in midsentence and smiled back at her. "Forgive me. I don't normally make speeches so early in the day." He bent down, pressed a light kiss to her forehead. "I'll be back in a minute, sweetheart. I just want to talk with Tom."

Who was Tom? she wondered. More importantly, who was this man who spoke with such conviction of the past? This man who'd taken to calling her "sweetheart"? It was far too soon for him to address her that way. She could tell him that, but it would have seemed silly, even prissy, and what was there in a word, anyway? He'd probably called a hundred other women "sweetheart." Set a hundred other women's hearts to beating high and fast in their throats.

Taken them away with him, as he was taking her.

But she wasn't those other women. She wasn't going to let anything happen between them. This was just a trip. A chance for her to discuss business with Nick. Business, she reminded herself when he came back into the cabin, sat on the sofa and drew her down beside him.

"We'll be in the air in a few minutes."

"Good," she said, and cleared her throat. "Who's Tom?"

"The pilot." Nick laced his fingers through hers. "I'm usually up there in the cockpit. But today I decided I'd rather be back here, with you."

"Ah," she said with a little smile. "So the prince sits beside his pilot and makes him nervous, hmm?"

He grinned. "The prince sits beside his *co*-pilot and flies the plane himself."

"You know how to fly?"

Nick settled back, put his feet up on the low table before the sofa and nodded. "I learned when I was just a kid. Distances are so vast in Quidar…flying is the easiest way to get from place to place."

"My stepbrothers say the same thing."

"It's the logical thing to do, especially when you're expected to put in appearances."

"Expected?"

"Uh-huh. It was one of my earliest responsibilities back home. Standing in for my father."

Amanda tried to imagine a boy with silver eyes taking on the burden of representing an absolute monarch.

"Back home. You mean, in Quidar."

"Yes." He lifted her hand, brought it to his mouth and brushed his lips over her knuckles. "I've spent a lot of my life in the States. My mother kept a home in California even after she married my father. But Quidar has always been 'home'. What about you?''

"Don't..." Her breath hitched. "Nick, don't do that.''

His brows rose. "Don't ask about your childhood?''

She made a sound she hoped would pass for a laugh. "Don't do—what you're doing. Kissing my hand. You said you wouldn't. You said—''

"You're right.'' He closed his fingers over hers, then put her hand in her lap and folded his arms. ''Tell me about yourself. Where is home for you?''

Her hand tingled. She could almost feel the warmth of his mouth still on her skin.

"I don't really think of anyplace as 'home','' she said briskly. "I was born in Chicago, but my parents were divorced when I was ten.'' *Why had she stopped him from holding her hand? There was nothing sexual in it.*

"And?''

"And,'' she said, even more briskly, ''my mother got a job in St. Louis, so we moved there. After a year or so, she sent us—my two sisters and me—to boarding school. We'd go to visit her some holidays and my father on others.'' *Take my hand, Nick. It was silly telling you not to. I like the feel of your fingers entwined with mine.* "So, when I think of 'home','' she said, stumbling a little on the words, ''sometimes it's Chicago. Sometimes it's St. Louis. Sometimes it's Connecticut, where I went to school. And there are times it's Dallas, where I lived when I was married.''

"What was he like? Your husband?''

"Like my father,'' she said, and laughed. ''I didn't realize it, of course, when I married him, but he was. Self-centered, removed...I don't think he ever thought of anyone but himself.'' Her breath hitched. Nick had taken her hand again. He was playing with her fingers, examining them as if they were new and remarkable objects.

"Did you love him?''

She blinked. He'd lifted his head. He was looking at her now, not at her hand, and he was still smiling, but the smile was false. She could see the tautness in his face, the glint of ice in his silver eyes.

"I thought I did. I mean, I wouldn't have married him if I—"

"Do you still?"

"No. Actually, I don't think I ever really...Nick? You're hurting my hand."

Nick looked at their joined hands. "Sorry," he said quickly, "I just—I..." He frowned, wondered why it should matter if Amanda Benning still carried the torch for her ex, then answered the question by telling himself he wouldn't want to bed any woman if she was still thinking about another man. "Sorry," he said again, and let go of her hand. "So." His tone was brisk, his smile polite. "You left Dallas and moved east. That must have been quite a change."

Amanda smiled. "Not as big a change as it must have been for you, going from Quidar to New York."

"Well, I spent lots of time in the States, growing up. And I went to school here." His smile softened. "But you're right. New York is nothing like Quidar."

"What's it like? Your country?"

He hesitated. Did she really want to hear about the desert, about the jagged mountains to the north and the sapphire sea to the south? She looked as if she did and, slowly, he began telling her about his homeland, and the wild beauty of it.

"I'm boring you," he said after he'd been talking for a long time.

"Oh, no." She reached for his hand, curled her fingers around his. "You're not. It sounds magnificent. Where do you live when you're there? In the desert, or in the mountains?"

So he told her more, about Zamidar and the Ivory Palace set against the backdrop of the mountains, about the scented gardens that surrounded it, about long summer nights in the endless expanse of the desert.

He told her more than he'd ever told anyone about his homeland and, he suddenly realized, about himself. And when he fell silent and she looked at him, her golden eyes shining, her lips bowed in a smile, and said Quidar must be incredibly beautiful, he came close to saying yes, it was. Very beautiful, and he longed to show it to her.

At that moment, the phone beside him buzzed. He picked it up, listened to his pilot give him an update on their speed and the projected time of arrival. He let out his breath and knew he'd never been so grateful to hear such dry statistics. The interruption had come at just the right time. Who knew what he might have said, otherwise?

The path back to reality lay in the sheaf of papers he knew he'd find inside the leather briefcase on the table beside him.

Carefully, he let go of Amanda's hand, reached for the case and opened it. "Forgive me," he said politely. "But I have a lot of reading to do before we reach our destination."

She nodded. "You don't have to explain," she said, just as politely. "I understand."

She didn't. He could see that in the way she shifted away from him. He'd hurt her. Embarrassed her. Taking his hand was the first gesture she'd made toward him and he'd rejected it.

Nick frowned and stared at the papers in his lap as if he really gave a damn about what they said. He was the one who'd direct their relationship. He would make no move unless she made it clear that was what she wanted, but inevitably, the start—and the finish—of an affair was up to him. It had always been that way, would always be that way.

Nick stopped thinking. He reached out, put his arm around Amanda's shoulders and drew her close.

"Come here," he said a little gruffly. "Put your head on my shoulder and keep me company while I wade through this stuff."

"Really, Nick, it's all right. I don't want to distract you."

"It's too late to worry about that," he said with a little laugh. "Sorry. I just—I have some things on my mind, that's all."

"Second thoughts about this trip?" she said, her tone stiff.

"Yes," he said bluntly, "but not about you."

"I don't understand."

"No, I don't, either." She looked up at him, her eyes filled with questions, and he sighed. "My brain is in a fog. Thinking about you kept me awake most of the night."

"That makes it unanimous."

"Well, why don't you take a nap, sweetheart? It'll take a few hours for us to get to Texas."

Amanda lifted her eyebrows. "Is that whe-ah we're a'goin'?" she said in a lazy drawl. "To Tex-as?"

Nick groaned. "That's terrible," he said, and grinned at her.

Amanda grinned back. "It's the best I can do. I'm not a native Texan."

"Better watch that phony accent." He touched the tip of her nose with his finger. "Our host is known for having a temper."

She yawned and burrowed closer, inhaled the scent of him. "Must be a Texas tradition. He can't have more of a temper than my stepfather. Are we going to a ranch? Is that why you told me to pack jeans?"

"Clever woman." She was cuddled up to him like a kitten, all warm, soft and sweet-smelling. Nick turned his head, buried his nose in her silken hair. "Yes. We're going to a ranch."

"Oh, that's nice," she said, and gave another delicate yawn. "It is?"

"Uh-huh. Maybe we'll get the chance to go riding. I like horses. And I love to ride."

"Do you?" Nick said, knowing he was grinning like an idiot. "Like to ride, I mean?"

"Mmm."

"I do, too. My father breeds Arabian horses. They're an ancient breed. Graceful, fast—"

"Mmm. I know something about Arabians."

He smiled. "Really?"

"Arabian horses," she said, and laughed. Her warm breath tickled his throat. "My stepfather has a weakness for them."

"Well, so does the owner of the ranch we're going to. My

father shipped a stallion to him, but something must have gone wrong during the flight.''

"Where is this ranch? What part of Texas?"

"It's near Austin. Do you know the area?"

"A little. I've spent some time there. My mother and step-father live nearby.''

Nick put the briefcase aside, leaned back and gathered Amanda closer. He didn't much care about reading through the papers Abdul had provided. Not right now. All he wanted to do was enjoy the feel of Amanda, nestled in his arms.

"Perhaps they're familiar with the ranch we're going to.''

"What's it called?" She smiled. "The Bar Something, right?"

Nick grinned and kissed her temple. "Wrong. It's called Espada.''

Her body, so soft and sweetly pliant seconds ago, became rigid in his embrace.

"Espada?" She sat straight up and stared at him. "We're going to Espada?''

"Yes. Do you know it?''

"Do I...?" Amanda barked a laugh, pulled free of his arms and shot to her feet. "Yes, I know it. For heaven's sake, Nick! Jonas Baron owns Espada.''

"Right. He's the man we're going to see.''

"Jonas is married to my mother.''

It took a minute for the message to sink in. "You mean—you mean, he's your stepfather?''

Amanda chuffed out a breath. "That's exactly what I mean.''

Nick couldn't believe it. How could something like this have happened? The irony was incredible. He'd never taken a woman with him on a business trip until today—and now, his business trip was taking Amanda straight into the bosom of her family.

No, he thought, and bit back a laugh. No, it was impossible. He never got involved with the families of the women he dated. Oh, he met mothers and fathers from time to time. You couldn't live the life he did and not have that happen. New York seemed like a big city to outsiders but the truth was that the inner circle, made up of financiers and industrialists, politicians and public figures, was surprisingly small.

After a while, the Joneses knew the Smiths and the Smiths knew the Browns and the Browns, of course, knew the Joneses. The names and faces all took on an almost stultifying familiarity.

But that wasn't the same as spending a weekend—a weekend, for God's sake—with a woman's parents.

He'd always been scrupulously careful about that. He'd turned down simple invitations to spend days in the country or on Long Island if it meant Daddy or Mommy would be there, and it hadn't a thing to do with anything as simple as the propriety—or the impropriety—of sharing the bed of the daughter of the house.

It had to do with far more delicate matters.

Family weekends were complications. They were far too personal. They created expectations he never, ever intended to fulfill.

"Dammit, Nick, say something! Didn't you hear what I said?"

He looked at Amanda. She was standing in front of him, her hands on her hips.

"Yes," he said slowly, as he rose to his feet. "I heard you."

"Well, I can't go there. To Espada. You'll have to tell Tim—"

"Tom," he said as if it mattered.

"I don't care what the pilot's name is!" She could hear her voice rising and she took a deep breath, told herself to calm down. "Nick, I'm sorry, but you'll have to take me back to New York. Or—or have your pilot—have Tom—land at an airport, any airport. I can take a commercial flight back to—"

"Amanda." He took her hands. "Take it easy."

"Take it easy?" She snorted, looked at him as if he were out of his mind. "Do you know what they'll think if I show up with you? Do you have any idea what my mother will— what Jonas will... Oh, God!''

She swung away. Nick caught her, drew her to him and wrapped his arms tightly around her. She was stiff and unyielding, but he didn't care. If anything, that was all the more reason to hold her close.

''They'll think we didn't want to be apart,'' he said roughly.

''Nick—''

''They'll think we just met and yes it's crazy, but the thought of being away from each other, even for a couple of days, was impossible.''

''Nick,'' she said again, but this time her voice was soft and her eyes were shining when she lifted her face to his.

''They'll think I'm the luckiest man in the world,'' he whispered, and then her arms were around his neck, her mouth was pressed to his, and nothing mattered to either of them but the joy and the wonder of the moment.

CHAPTER NINE

THE afternoon sun was high in the western sky as Marta Baron settled into her chair on the upper level of her waterfall deck, smiled politely at her guests and wondered what on earth she was supposed to say to the stranger who was her daughter's lover.

At least, she assumed Sheikh Nicholas al Rashid was Amanda's lover.

It hadn't been a very difficult assumption to make.

The expression on the sheikh's handsome face when he looked at Amanda, the way he kept his arm possessively around her waist, even the softness in his voice when he used her name, were all dead giveaways.

He might as well have been wearing a sign that read, This Woman Belongs To Me.

Amanda was harder to read.

There was a delicate pink flush to her cheeks, and she had a way of glancing at the sheikh as if they were alone on the planet, but Marta thought she'd noticed an angry snap in her daughter's eyes when the sheikh's arm had closed around her—a look he had studiously ignored as he drew her down beside him on the cushioned teak glider.

"...so I said, well, why would I want to buy a horse from a man who couldn't tell the front end of a jackass from the rear?" Jonas said, and Marta laughed politely, along with everybody else.

She'd always considered herself a sophisticated woman, even before she'd assumed her duties as the wife of Jonas Baron. She'd lived through the sexual revolution, looked the other way when her girls were in college and one or the other of them had brought a boy home for the weekend. Not that

121

she'd put them in one room, but she'd known that closed doors hadn't kept them from sleeping—or not sleeping, she thought wryly—in the same bed.

Not Amanda, though.

Marta smiled at something the sheikh said, but her attention was focused on her middle daughter.

Amanda had never brought a boy home. She'd never brought a man home, either; surely that ex-husband of hers didn't qualify. He'd been a self-serving, emotionless phony. Marta had only figured out why Amanda married him after the marriage ended, when she realized her daughter had been looking for the father she'd never really had.

Marta lifted her glass of iced tea and took a delicate sip.

One thing was certain. No one could ever mistake Sheikh Nicholas al Rashid for a father figure. He was, to use the indelicate parlance of the day, a hunk.

And she had to stop thinking of him as Sheikh.

"Please," he'd said, lifting her hand to his lips, "call me Nick."

She looked at him, seated beside Amanda. He was watching Jonas, listening to him, but his concentration was on the woman at his side. There was no mistaking the deliberate brush of that hard-looking shoulder against hers, the flex of his hand along her hip.

If Nick and Amanda weren't yet lovers, they would be, and soon. This was a man who always got what he wanted, and he wanted Amanda. But would he know what to do with her once he had her?

No, Marta thought, he wouldn't.

Nick was like a much younger version of her own husband. He was strong, powerful and determined. He was also, she was certain, often unyielding and immovable. A successful monarch needed those traits to run his empire—Jonas to rule Espada, Nick to rule Quidar.

Men like that were difficult to deal with. They could break a woman's heart with terrifying ease. It didn't help that they also attracted women as readily as nectar attracted hummingbirds. And because men were men, they'd always want the freshest little flower with the brightest petals.

Marta sighed.

She waged a constant battle against time's cruel ravages, but, paradoxically enough, time was her ally in matters of the heart. She'd come along late enough in Jonas's life so that she could be fairly certain she was the last woman he'd want to taste. It wasn't an especially sentimental view but it was a realistic, even reassuring one, because she loved her husband and would never willingly have given him up.

Amanda was enough like her so that she'd love the same way, once she found the man she really wanted. Marta could only hope Nick wasn't that man. He had the look about him of a man who would love one woman with heart-stopping intensity, but only on his terms.

For a woman like her daughter, that would not work.

Amanda, Marta thought, Amanda, sweetie, what are you doing?

"...have known it instantly, Mrs. Baron, even if we'd met accidentally."

Marta blinked. Nick was smiling at her, but she had no idea what he'd said.

"Sorry, Your Highness—"

"Nick, please."

"Nick." Marta smiled, too. "I'm afraid I missed that."

"I said, I'd have known you were Amanda's mother even if no one told me. You look enough alike to pass as sisters."

"And you must have a bit of Irish in your blood," Marta said, her smile broadening, "to be able to spout such blarney without laughing."

Nick grinned. "It's the truth, Mrs. Baron, though, actually, my mother always claimed she had an Irish grandfather."

"Please. Call me Marta. Yes, now that you mention it, I think I've read that your mother was American."

"She was, and proud of it, as I am proud of my American half. I've always felt very fortunate to be the product of two such extraordinary cultures."

"One foot in the past," Marta said, still smiling, "and one in the future. Which suits you best, I wonder?"

"Mother," Amanda said, but Nick only chuckled.

"Both have their advantages. So far, I've never found it necessary to choose one over the other."

"No. Why would you, when you can have the best of both worlds? Here you are, blue jeans and all—"

"It's difficult to handle horses in a suit," Nick said, and smiled.

Marta smiled, too. "You know what I mean, Nick. Any time you wish, you're free to turn into the ruler of your own kingdom, do as you will, come and go as you please, answering to no one."

"Mother, for heaven's sake—"

"No." Nick took his arm from around Amanda, lifted her hand to his mouth and kissed it. "No, your mother's quite right. Perhaps it's a simplification, but it's pretty much an accurate description of my life." He rose to his feet. "Marta? I noticed a garden behind the house. Would you be kind enough to walk me through it?"

"Of course." Marta rose, too. "Do you like flowers, Nick?"

"Yes," he said simply. "Especially those that are beautiful and have the strength to flourish in difficult climes."

Marta smiled and took his arm as they strolled down the steps, along the path and into the garden.

"There aren't many flowers that can manage that," she said after a few minutes.

"No, there aren't." Nick paused and turned toward her. "Let's not speak in metaphors, Marta. You don't like me, do you?"

"It isn't that I don't like you. It's..." Marta hesitated. "Look, I'm not old-fashioned. I'm not going to ask you what your intentions are with regard to my daughter."

"I'm glad to hear it." He spoke politely, but his words were edged with steel. "Because it's none of your business. Our relationship, Amanda's and mine, doesn't concern anyone but us.''

"I know. Like it or not, my little girl is all grown up. But her welfare does concern me. I don't want to see her hurt.''

Nick jammed his hands into the back pockets of his jeans. "And you think I do?''

"No, of course not. It's just… A man like you can hurt a woman unintentionally.''

"A man like me,'' he said coldly. "Just what is that supposed to mean?''

"Oh, I'm not trying to insult you…'' Marta gave a little laugh. "But I'm doing a fine job of it, aren't I?'' She put her hand lightly on his arm. "Nick, you remind me of my husband in so many ways. All the things that make you successful can be difficult for a woman to deal with.''

"Are you saying being successful is a drawback in a relationship?''

"On the contrary. It's a wonderful asset. But sometimes success can lead to a kind of selfishness.'' Marta clicked her tongue. "Just listen to me! I sound like one of those horrible newspaper advice columnists.'' She looped her arm through Nick's and drew him forward. "Jonas would tell me I'm meddling.''

"Well, he'd be right.'' Nick softened the words with a grin. "But I understand. You love your daughter. And I—I…'' God, what was he saying? "I can promise you, Marta, I care about her, too.''

"Good. And now, let me show you the vegetables I grow, way in the back garden. Tomatoes, actually. Hundred-dollar tomatoes, Jonas calls them.'' Marta smiled. "And, Nick? I'm very happy to have you here at Espada. Whatever happens, a woman should have at least one man in her life who looks at her the way you look at Amanda.''

"Every man who sees her must look at her that way,'' Nick said, and cleared his throat.

"Well, let me put that another way, then. I've never seen a man look at her the way you do.''

Nick stopped in his tracks. "Not even her husband?"

Marta shook her head. "Especially not her husband."

"He must have been an idiot."

Marta laughed. "What a perceptive man you are, Nicholas al Rashid!"

Nick spent most of the remaining afternoon at the stables with Jonas, the ranch foreman and the vet. By evening, he was satisfied that the Arabian stallion was suffering from nothing more serious than a minor sprain and a major case of nerves.

"Who could possibly blame him?" Nick had said when he'd come back up to the house. "He's gone from Quidar to Texas. That's a one-hundred-eighty-degree change in any life."

A one-hundred-eighty-degree change indeed, Amanda thought as she slipped into the emerald-green dress Marta had loaned her to wear for dinner.

Before last night, the only thing she'd known about Nick was that she didn't like him. She liked him now, though. More than was reasonable or logical...or safe.

Her mother had tried to tell her that when she'd brought her the dress and a matching pair of shoes.

"Good thing we're about the same size," Marta had said with a smile. "Not that you don't look charming in denim, but Jonas likes to dress for dinner. He'd never admit it, of course. He lays the blame on me."

Amanda sighed. "I just wish I hadn't listened to Nick when he told me to pack nothing but jeans."

"A good thing his valet didn't." Marta grinned. "That was a delightful story the sheikh told, about unpacking his bag and finding a dark suit tucked in with his riding boots."

"Mmm. That was probably the work of his secretary. That's what Nick calls him anyway, this funny little man who bows himself in and out of rooms."

Marta plucked a loose thread from the dress's hem. "Well, after all, sweetie, Nick is heir to the throne of Quidar."

Amanda held the dress up against herself and looked in the mirror. "It's perfect. Thanks, Mom."

"I gather you didn't even know you were coming to Espada."

"No. Nick didn't mention it. He just said we were flying somewhere."

"And you said you'd go with him."

Was that a gentle note of censure in her mother's voice? Color rose in Amanda's cheeks as the women's eyes met in the mirror.

"Yes. Yes, I did."

"And no wonder. He's a fascinating young man. Charming, intelligent, Incredibly good-looking. And, I would think, very accustomed to getting his own way." Marta smiled. "Actually, he reminds me of Jonas."

Amanda turned around. "Nothing's going on between us," she said flatly.

"Oh, I think you're wrong, sweetie. I think a lot is going on. You just aren't ready to admit it."

"Mom—"

"You don't owe me any explanations, darling. You're a grown woman. And I have every confidence in your ability to make your own decisions." Marta reached for her daughter's hands and clasped them tightly. "I just don't want to see you get hurt."

"Nick would never—"

"There are different ways of being hurt, Mandy. Loving a man who may not be able to love you back in quite the same way is perhaps the worst pain of all."

"I don't love Nick! I admit, I'm—I'm infatuated with him, but—"

Marta had smiled and put her finger over Amanda's lips. "Go on," she'd said gently, "make yourself beautiful for your young man."

Beautiful? Amanda thought as she finished dressing. She wondered if Nick would think so. There'd certainly been more stunning women at the party last night, and she'd never be an eye-catching knockout like Deanna Burgess.

But she wanted Nick to like what he saw tonight. Any woman would. That didn't mean she was in love with him…

And then she opened her door to Nick's polite knock and knew, without any hesitancy, that she was. Everything her mother had said was true.

"Hi."

"Hi yourself." Her heartbeat stuttered. Amanda took a breath, dredged up a smile. "You're right on time."

"Always."

He grinned, and she wondered frantically how it could have happened. She hadn't been looking to fall in love. And if she had, it wouldn't have been with the Lion of the Desert.

"My father drummed it into me."

"What?"

"The importance of being on time. Sort of the eleventh commandment. You know, 'Thou shalt never be late.'"

"Yes." She swallowed dryly, fought to hang on to whatever remained of her composure. *How? How could she have fallen in love so quickly?* "Well, it worked. You're certainly prompt."

His smile tilted. "And you," he said softly, "are incredibly beautiful."

His words, the velvet softness of them, even the way he was looking at her, ignited a slow-burning heat in her bones.

"Thank you. It's my mother's dress. I didn't—"

"I know. I should have anticipated that the Barons would expect us to dine with them." A muscle danced in his jaw. He moved toward her, his eyes a burnished silver. "But I didn't think of anything except you. Since last night I haven't been able to think of anything but you."

"Nick…"

Gently, he took her face in his hands, lifted it to his. He could feel her trembling with the same excitement that burned inside him.

"One kiss," he said softly, "just one, before we go down-stairs."

"All right. Just—"

His mouth closed over hers. Amanda moaned, closed her eyes, lifted her hands and laid them against his chest. His heart was racing, but no faster than hers. She moved closer to him, closer still, and he swept his arms around her, gathered her against him so that she could feel his hunger.

"Nick," she said in a choked whisper, "oh, Nick..."

He took her hand from his chest, brought it down his body, cupped it over his arousal. He groaned, or maybe it was she who made that soft, yearning sound. It didn't matter. Her needs, and his, were the same.

"To hell with dinner," he whispered. "Amanda, I want to touch you. To undress you. To bury myself inside you while you lift your arms to me and cry out my name."

"Oh, yes! It's what I want, too." She took a shaky breath, lifted her hand from the heat and hardness of him and leaned back in his arms. "But Jonas and Marta expect us to join them."

Nick bent his head, nipped gently at her throat. "I don't give a damn what they want."

Amanda gave a breathless laugh. "Nick, that's my mother downstairs."

He laughed, too, or made the attempt. "I'm sorry, sweetheart. Of course it is. Okay. Just give me a minute. Then we'll make our entrance, pretend we're interested in drinks and dinner and polite conversation for a couple of hours—"

"Only for a couple of hours."

He tugged her towards him and she went willingly, thrust her hands into his hair, dragged his mouth down to hers and kissed him.

Nick felt the kiss pierce his heart like an arrow.

A couple of hours, he'd said. Since when could a couple of hours seem like an eternity?

Drinks first, out on the deck, where they were joined by

Tyler and Caitlin Kincaid. They lived nearby, Jonas said. He clapped Tyler on the back, gave him a proud smile and said Tyler was his son and Caitlin his stepdaughter.

Any other time, Nick would have found that intriguing. A son who didn't bear the old man's name. A stepdaughter, but obviously not of Marta's blood. Interesting, he thought—but then his curiosity faded.

His only interest was Amanda.

Still, he went through the motions. Made pleasant small talk. Murmured something about the excellence of the wine. Agreed that dinner was a masterpiece. He supposed it was. Everybody said so. The thing was, he couldn't taste any of it.

Nothing had any flavor. How could it, when the only taste that mattered was Amanda's? That last kiss lingered on his mouth. The memory of it. The way she'd pulled his head down to hers, the way she'd initiated that all-consuming, hungry kiss...

Ah, hell. Nick shifted uneasily in his chair.

He was too old for this. Boys worried about their hormones making them look foolish, and he was far from being a boy. But just thinking about her...the heat of her in his arms; the sweet sounds she made when he kissed her; the way she fitted herself against him...

Hell, he thought again, and cleared his throat.

"...oil strike?"

He blinked, looked around the table blindly. Everyone was looking at him.

"Sorry," he said, and cleared his throat again. "Tyler? Did you say something?"

"I was just wondering about that oil strike in Quidar last year. Was it really the gusher our people said it was?"

"Oh. Oh, yeah. Absolutely. The field was huge, bigger than..."

Nick talked about oil. He talked about oil prices. And all the time part of his brain was doing such sensible things, another part was wondering what Amanda was thinking. She was seated beside him, and every now and then when he trusted himself to do it without pulling her into his arms, he looked at her. Her golden eyes were wide; her cheeks were flushed. And when he took her hand under the table, he could feel her tremble.

Was she aching, as he was, for these endless hours to pass so that she could come into his arms and ask him to take her? Because she had to ask. He'd told her that she had to ask, and he was a man of his word, would remain a man of his word, even if it killed him. It would, if he didn't have her. If he didn't make her his.

"Nick?"

And if any son of a bitch tried to take her from him, he'd—

"Nick?"

Nick frowned. They were on the deck again, just he and Tyler Kincaid, though he had only the haziest recollection of finishing dessert and agreeing it would be great to go outside for a breath of air.

"Yes." Nick inhaled deeply, then let out his breath. "Kincaid. Tyler. I…hell, I'm sorry. You must think I'm—"

"What I think," Tyler said with wry amusement, "is that if you and Amanda don't get behind a closed door pretty damn soon, the rest of us are going to be in for an extremely interesting night."

Nick swung toward him, eyes narrowed. "What's that supposed to mean, Kincaid?"

"It means that the temperature goes up a hundred degrees each time you look at each other," Tyler said carefully. "And that if you think you'd rather work it off by taking me on, you're welcome to try it."

The two men stared at each other and then Nick gave a choked laugh. "Sorry. Damn, I'm sorry. I just—"

"Yeah. I know the feeling." Tyler leaned back against the deck rail. "Amazing, isn't it? What falling in love with a woman can do to a perfectly normal, completely sensible male?"

"In…?" Nick shook his head. "You've got it wrong. I'm not—"

"Tyler?" Caitlin Kincaid smiled as she came toward them. "Tyler, darling, it's late. We really should be leaving. It was lovely meeting you, Nick."

"Yes." Nick took her hand and brought it to his lips. "I gave your husband my card. Give me a call the next time you're in New York."

Caitlin rose on her toes and kissed his cheek. "I think it's wonderful," she whispered.

Nick felt bewildered as she stepped back into the arc of her husband's arm. "What's wonderful?"

Tyler looked at Nick, started to say something, then thought better of it. "Well," he said, and held out his hand, "it's been a pleasure meeting you."

"Yeah," Nick said. "Uh, Tyler? You're definitely wrong. About what you said. I mean, I'm not—I'm certainly not—"

"Of course you're not," Tyler said solemnly.

Nick thought he heard Kincaid chuckle as he and his wife walked into the house. Not that it mattered. The laugh was on Tyler if he thought any rational man would ever confuse lust with love.

After a while, the lights in the house went off. He straightened up, looked at the lighted dial of his watch. How long had he been out here? Had Amanda gone to her room? Had he misread what he'd seen in her eyes all evening?

"Nick?"

He turned and saw her standing in the doorway, a beautiful shadow in the soft light of the moon. The sight of her almost stopped his heart, but then, desire—lust—could be a powerful thing. Any thinking man knew that.

"Nick," she said again, and Nicholas al Rashid, the Lion of the Desert, stopped thinking, went to the woman he wanted, the woman he'd always wanted since the beginning of time, took her in his arms and kissed her again and again until he could no longer tell where she left off and he began.

CHAPTER TEN

THE world was spinning out of control, the stars racing across the black Texas sky like a kaleidoscope gone mad.

"Tell me, sweetheart." Nick's voice was hoarse and urgent. "Tell me what you want."

Amanda looked up at this man who'd turned her life upside down, this dangerous, gorgeous, complex stranger, and framed his face with her hands. "You," she said softly. "I want—"

Nick's mouth closed hungrily over hers. His hands slipped down her spine, cupped her bottom, lifted her into his heat and hardness.

Desire sparkled in her blood. She moaned, caught his lip between her teeth, bit gently into the soft flesh and traced the tiny wound with the tip of her tongue. His arms tightened around her and he whispered something in a language she couldn't understand, but words didn't matter.

Not now.

Nick drew back, just enough so he could see Amanda's face in the pearlescent glow of the moon.

"You're so beautiful," he whispered, and kissed her again, heating her mouth with his, parting it with his, feasting on the taste of her, on the little sounds she made as she returned his kisses. She was trembling in his arms, straining against him, fitting her body to his until nothing but the whisper of their clothing separated them.

Nick knew he couldn't take much more of this sweet torment.

The moon slipped behind the surrounding hills. The silver-shot night swooped down, embraced them in a cloak of velvet darkness.

He drew Amanda closer, settled her in the inverted vee of

his legs. His erection pressed against her belly and she sighed his name.

"Please," she whispered, "Nick, please..."

"Amanda." His voice was raw. "Sweetheart, come upstairs with me."

"Please," she said again, and kissed him, took his tongue into her mouth, and he was lost.

He bunched the silk of her skirt in his fists and pushed it up her thighs. She was wearing stockings and a small triangle of silk. His brain registered that much and, in some still-functioning part of it, he thought about how exciting it would be to see her now, see those long, elegant legs, that scrap of silk, but then she moved her hips and he forgot everything but the uncontrollable need to possess her.

"Amanda," he groaned, and he slipped his hand between her thighs and cupped her, felt the heat of her, and the dampness. He moved against her, moved again, and she moaned.

She slid her hands up his chest, shoved his jacket half off his shoulders, fumbled at his tie, at the buttons of his shirt, and put her hands on his skin. She felt her knees go weak. Oh, the feel of him! The hot male skin. The whorls of silky hair, the ridges of hard muscle.

Nick caught her hands, held them against the thudding beat of his heart.

"Amanda." He dragged air into his lungs, told himself to breathe, to think, to slow down. He'd waited all these years for this moment. He knew it now, knew that he'd lived with the memory of the woman in his arms since he'd first seen her. Now, at last, she would be his—but not like this.

She was as soft as the petals of a rosebud, as lovely as a dream. He wanted to pleasure her slowly, take her slowly, see her eyes turn blind with passion as he took her to the brink of ecstasy over and over again before they tumbled over the edge and fell through time, joined together for eternity.

Nick shuddered.

Unless she moved against him. Yes, like that. Unless she lifted herself to him like that. Just like that. Unless her delicate tongue searched for his. Unless she rubbed her hot, feminine core against his palm…

A cry broke from his throat. He drew her closer into his embrace, deeper into the inky silence of the moonless night, and pressed her back against the railing.

"Look at me," he whispered, and when her eyes met his, he ripped away the bit of silk between her thighs, found the tiny bud that bloomed there. Touched her. Stroked her. And kissed her, kissed her and drank in her cries as she came against his hand.

She sobbed his name, pulled down his zipper, found him, held him, stroked him, and then, oh then, she was a hot silken fist taking him deep inside her.

Nick strove for sanity. Wait for her, he told himself, dammit, wait.

Amanda trembled and arched like a bow in his arms, tore her mouth from his and sank her teeth into his shoulder. The sound, the feel, the heat of her surrender finished him. He stopped thinking, slid his hand around the nape of her neck, took her mouth with his and exploded deep within her satin walls.

For long moments, neither of them moved. Then Nick let out a breath, pulled down her skirt and gently kissed her lips. "Sweetheart," he whispered.

She shook her head, made a weak little sound and tried to turn her face from his, but he caught her chin, kissed her again and tasted the salt of her tears.

Nick cursed, damned himself for being such a selfish fool. He enfolded her even more closely in his arms, cupped her head and brought it to his shoulder.

"Forgive me, sweetheart," he murmured, rocking her gently in his embrace. "I know it was too quick. I meant to go slowly, to make it perfect."

Amanda lifted her head, silenced him with a kiss. "It *was* perfect."

"But you're crying."

She gave a soft little laugh. "I know. It's just…" *It's just that my heart is full,* she thought. Full with love, for the first time in her life. She smiled, put her hand to his cheek. "Those weren't sad tears," she whispered. "This was—what we just did—I've never..."

He felt his heart swell with joy. "Never?"

She shook her head. "Never."

He kissed her again until she was breathless with desire. Then he put his arm around her, led her into the sleeping house and took her, at last, to bed.

Amanda awoke to Nick's kisses just before dawn.

"Hello, sweetheart," he whispered.

Safe and warm in the curve of his arm, she smiled up at him. "Good morning."

He bent to her, kissed her mouth with lingering tenderness. "You slept in my arms all night."

"Mmm."

"I liked having you there."

"Mmm," she said again, and laced her fingers into his dark hair.

He smiled, nipped gently at her bottom lip. "You're not a morning conversationalist, huh?"

Amanda laughed softly. "I'm not a morning anything. I don't... " Her breath hitched. "Nick?"

"You see, sweetheart?" His voice roughened as he caressed her breast, licked the nipple and watched it bead. "It isn't true that you're not a morning anything. You just need to find something that appeals to you."

She caught her breath, lifted herself to his mouth.

"Like this for instance. Or..." He shifted, moved farther down her warm flesh and gently parted her thighs. "Or this."

He loved the soft sound she made as he put his mouth against her, loved the sweet taste of her, like honey on his tongue. And the scent of her, of aroused woman, filled him with hot pleasure. How could he want her again? He'd had her endless times during the long, miraculous night.

But he would never have her enough, he thought suddenly,

and he rose above her, looked down into her passion-flushed face and spoke her name.

Her lashes flew up. Her wide golden eyes looked into his as he entered her and he saw the blur of pleasure suffuse her face. He withdrew, slid into her again, drove deeper, saw her eyes darken and her lips form his name.

"Yes," he whispered, "yes," and he caught her hands, laced his fingers through hers and stretched her arms to the sides, still moving, still seeking not just that incredible moment when they would fly into the sun together but something more, something he'd never known.

"Nick," she moaned, just that, only that, but he could hear—he thought he could hear—everything a man could hope for, long for, in the way she said his name.

"Come with me," he said, "Amanda, love..."

She wrapped her legs around his hips, sobbed his name, and Nick stopped thinking, stopped wondering, and lost himself in the woman in his arms.

Afterward, they lay in a warm, contented tangle, her head on his chest, his arms holding her close.

He gave a dramatic groan. "I'm never going to be able to move again."

She laughed softly, propped her chin on her wrist and looked at him. "Be sure and explain that to the housekeeper when she finds your naked body in my bed."

"I'll just smile and tell her that I died and went to heaven."

"Uh-huh. My mother will probably love that explanation."

"Hell," Nick grumbled. She squealed as he rolled her onto her back, gently drew her hands above her head and manacled them with his. "Let me be sure I understand this, Ms. Benning. You expect me to get up, get dressed and beat it back to my room before the sun rises." He bent his head, kissed her mouth. "Is there no pity in your heart for a man who's given his all?"

Amanda gave a little hum of satisfaction. "But you haven't given your all," she said huskily, and shifted beneath him. "Or am I imagining things?"

"What?" Nick said with mock indignation. "You can't be referring to this."

"But I am."

And then, neither of them was laughing.

"Amanda," he whispered, "sweetheart."

He drew her into his arms and they made love again, slowly, exploring each other, tasting each other, coming at last to a climax no less transcendent for all the sweet, gentle steps that had led them to it.

Nick held Amanda close for long moments, savoring the slowing beat of her heart against his. How could he have thought he knew what sex was, when he'd lived without ever knowing this sense of completion in a woman's arms?

He'd been with many women, all of them beautiful, almost all of them skilled in bed. Amanda was beautiful, yes. And she was eager, even wild in his arms, but skill...?

He drew her more tightly into his embrace.

She wasn't skilled. There'd been moments during the night when she'd caught her breath at some of the things he'd done. "Oh," she'd whispered once, "Nick, I never..."

Shall I stop? he'd said, even though stopping would have half killed him, but there was nothing he wouldn't do to please her. And she'd sighed and touched him and said no, please, no, don't ever stop.

Which, he thought, staring up at the ceiling, just about terrified him. Because he didn't want to stop. Not ever. Not just making love to her, although he suspected he could do that for the rest of his life without ever tiring of it.

The thing of it was, he didn't want to stop being with Amanda. Laughing with her. Talking with her. Even arguing with her. He didn't want any of that to stop.

And it scared the hell out of him.

What was happening here? He'd met this woman less than two days ago under what could only charitably be called suspicious circumstances. He didn't know very much about her. And now, he was thinking—he felt as if he might be—he had this idea that—

Nick slid his arm from beneath Amanda's shoulders and sat up.

"It's getting late," he said, and flashed a quick smile as he got out of bed, stepped into his trousers and pulled on his shirt. "The sun's coming up."

"Nick?" Amanda shifted against the pillow, rose on her elbows and looked at him. "What's the matter?"

"Nothing. Nothing's the matter. I just, uh, I dropped a cuff link."

He bent down, collected the rest of the clothing he'd practically torn off last night, then searched the carpet vigilantly for a cuff link that had gone astray. It was much easier to think he might have lost a cuff link than a far more vital part of himself, one he'd never given any woman—one he wasn't sure he could retrieve.

"Found it," he said, straightening up, holding out the link and smiling again as he quickly made his way to the door. "I'll see you at breakfast. Okay?"

She nodded, then drew the blanket to her chin. She looked lost and puzzled, and he came within a breath of dropping his stuff, going back to her and taking her in his arms.

"Go on," she said, "before you turn into a pumpkin. Or whatever it is sheikhs turn into when the moon goes down and the sun comes up. Dammit, Nick, I can smell coffee. Someone's awake, and I don't want them to find you here."

Her voice had taken on strength. She looked neither lost or puzzled, just annoyed. Annoyed, because he wasn't getting out of her room fast enough? Because someone might find him with her?

Nick's mouth thinned. What if he told her he damned well wasn't going anywhere? That he belonged in her bed just as she belonged in his arms?

"Will you please leave?"

"Of course," he said politely, and shut the door after him.

Amanda stared at the closed door. She wanted to roll over on her belly, clutch her pillow and weep. Instead, she grabbed the pillows, first his, then hers, and hurled them at the door.

What a fool she'd been, thinking this had been anything more than sex to Nick. And what a fool she'd been, thinking she was in love with him. She was far too intelligent to fall for a man like Nicholas al Rashid. What woman would want a man who could never love anyone as much as he loved himself?

This, she thought grimly, this was what he'd been after, all along. To sleep with her and add another conquest to his list.

She hadn't been a fool, she'd been an idiot.

No wonder he'd called off their wager. He'd known she'd sleep with him. After all, he was irresistible. He thought so, anyway. But why saddle himself with keeping her, or having her, or whatever the hell you called the responsibility a man like that assumed when he took a mistress?

Look at how easily he'd rid himself of Deanna. No second thoughts. No hesitation.

Amanda sucked in her breath. "Stop it," she said.

She rose quickly, stepped over the little pile of silky clothing that lay on the carpet. She wouldn't think about how Nick had undressed her, how they'd barely closed the door before he'd been pulling off his clothes and hers, arousing her so fast, so completely, that they'd only just made it to the bed before he was inside her again.

Don't look, she told herself hotly, not at the clothes, not at the mirror...

Too late.

She'd already turned, sought out her reflection in the glass and found a stranger. A woman with tousled hair and a kiss-swollen mouth. With the marks of a man's possession on her body.

There, on her mouth. At the juncture of shoulder and throat. On her thighs.

Amanda trembled.

Nick hadn't hurt her, but he'd marked her. Marked her as his own. No man had ever done that. Well, there'd only been one other man. Her husband. And his idea of sex had been something done quickly, almost clinically. Like—like brush-

ing your teeth. That was how she'd assumed it was supposed
to be. A couple of kisses, a fast, slightly uncomfortable pen-
etration.

How could she have known that making love could be wild
one moment and tender the next? That nothing in the world
could compare to what happened when you spun out of control
in the arms of your lover, and he came apart in yours?

Tears blurred her vision. She swung away from the mirror
and hurried into the bathroom.

What was done, was done. She didn't regret it. Why should
she? she thought, as she stepped into the shower. Actually, she
owed Nick a debt of gratitude for the night they'd spent together. He'd taught her things about herself, about her capacity
for passion and pleasure, she might never have known.

She turned off the water, reached for a towel and dried
herself briskly.

This wasn't some Victorian melodrama. She wasn't a virgin
whose innocence had been sullied. Neither was she a woman
who could possibly fall in love with a man in, what, forty-
eight hours? She'd only told herself that because facing the
truth—that she'd wanted to sleep with a stranger—had been
too difficult.

"Silly," she murmured, and looked into the mirror again
and smiled at her self-confident, coolly-contained reflection.

She dressed quickly in a silk T-shirt and jeans and went
down the stairs. Her mother was having coffee in the breakfast
room.

"Good morning, darling," Marta said. "Did you sleep
well?"

"Very well," Amanda replied. She could feel herself blush-
ing and she went straight to the buffet and poured herself
coffee. "Where's Jonas?"

Marta smiled. "Oh, he was up hours ago. He's outside
somewhere, probably driving his men crazy." She took a sip
of coffee. "Have you seen Nick?"

"No," Amanda said quickly. Too quickly. She saw her

mother's eyebrows lift. "I mean, how could I have seen him? He's probably still sleeping."

"He isn't," Marta said slowly. "Sweetie, he had a phone call a few minutes ago. I don't know what it was about, but he said he had to leave for home right away."

"Ah." Amanda smiled brightly, as if the news that he hadn't even wanted to say goodbye to her was meaningless. "I see. Well, that's no problem. I'll call the airport and book myself a seat—"

Strong hands closed on her shoulders. She gasped as Nick swung her toward him. His eyes were dark, his expression grim.

"Is that what you think of me?" he said coldly. "That I'd leave you without a word?"

"Yes," she said. Her voice trembled, but her chin was raised in defiance. "That's exactly what I thought."

Nick's mouth twisted. He wrapped his fingers around her wrist and started for the door. "Excuse us, please, Marta." He spoke politely, but there was no mistaking that the words weren't a request, they were a command.

"Amanda?" her mother said.

"It's all right, Mother."

It wasn't. Did Nick think he had to add to her humiliation by dragging her after him like a parcel? Amanda wrenched free of his grasp as soon as they were in the hall.

"Just who in hell do you think you are?" she said in an angry whisper. "Strolling out of my bedroom without so much as a look. Making some pathetic excuse so you can fly back to New York. Grabbing me as if you owned me, right in front of my mother—"

"I'm not flying back to New York."

"Frankly, Lord Rashid, I don't give a damn where you're—"

"I'm flying to Quidar. My father's having political problems. Serious ones."

Amanda folded her arms. As excuses went, this was a good one but then, a man who was the son of an absolute monarch wouldn't be reduced to pleading absence because of a sick grandmother.

"It's the truth."

It probably was. Nick might not have much loyalty to the women who warmed his bed, but she had no doubt that he was loyal to his king and to his kingdom.

"I'm sorry to hear it," she said stiffly.

"I'll be gone a week. Or a month. I can't be certain."

"You don't have to explain yourself to me, Your Highness."

"Dammit," Nick growled, clasping her elbows and lifting her to her toes, "what's the matter with you?"

"Nothing's the matter with me."

"Don't lie to me, Amanda."

"Why not? I asked you that same question a little while ago. Remember? 'What's the matter?' I said, and you gave me the answer I just gave you."

"Yeah, well, I lied." His hands tightened on her. "You want an answer? All right. I'll give you one." He took a deep breath. "I was afraid."

"Of what?"

"Of..." He let go of her, ran his hands through his hair. Color striped his cheekbones. "I don't know." He hesitated. "Dammit, I was afraid of you."

"The Lion of the Desert? Afraid of me?" She laughed and took a step back. "Nice try, Your Loftiness, but—"

Nick pulled her into his arms. "This isn't a game! I'm trying to tell you what happened to me this morning. When I kissed you, when I knew it was time to leave you..." His throat constricted. "Amanda." He drew her close, cupped her face and looked into her eyes. "Come with me."

"Come with you?"

"Yes. I don't want to leave you. I *can't* leave you." He kissed her, then looked into her eyes again. "Come with me, sweetheart."

"No!" Marta Baron's voice rang out like the hour bell from a campanile. Amanda spun around and saw her mother, standing in the entrance to the breakfast room. "Amanda, darling, don't go. Please. I have this feeling…"

"Amanda," Nick said softly, "I want you with me."

What was the good of pretending? Amanda turned to the man she loved. "And I want to be with you."

An hour later, they were in the air, en route to an ancient kingdom where the word of the Lion of the Desert was law.

CHAPTER ELEVEN

NICK wasted no time once Amanda said she'd go with him.

They were in the air in record time. Shortly after takeoff, he took out his cell phone and made a flurry of calls. Then he sat back and took Amanda's hand.

"Abdul will meet us in Quidar."

"You've asked Abdul to fly to Quidar?"

"Yes, of course. He's familiar with the situation back home. He's worked with me for years, and before me—"

"I know. Your father, and your grandfather, too."

"Exactly." Nick brought her hand to his mouth and kissed it. "You don't like Abdul, do you?"

"I don't know him well enough not to like him. It's just...I get the feeling he doesn't like me." Amanda looked at their joined hands, then at Nick. "I doubt if he'll be very happy when he sees you've brought me with you."

"He's my secretary. He's not required to think about anything other than his duties. My private life isn't his concern."

"You don't really believe that," she said with a little laugh. "Everything about you is Abdul's concern."

"No, sweetheart, you're wrong. The duties of the secretary to the heir to the throne are very clear. It is—"

"—the custom," Amanda said, more sharply than she'd intended.

"Yes. Such things are very important in my country."

"Customs. Duties. And rules."

"Sweetheart, don't look like that."

"Like what?" she said, and even she could hear the petulance in her voice.

Nick put his arm around her. "You'll like Quidar." He smiled. "At least, I hope you will."

Amanda sighed and let herself lean into him. "How long is the flight?"

"Too long for us to try to make it in this plane. We'd have to stop for refueling at least twice, and I don't want to waste the time. We'll board a commercial jet in Dallas. And..." He glanced at his watch. "And twelve hours from now, we'll step down on the soil of my homeland."

The soil of his homeland. A place called Quidar. A country so remote, so ancient, that it had only opened its borders to outsiders under the rule of Nick's father...

Amanda sat up straight. "Nick. I just realized I don't have my passport."

He smiled and reached for her hand. "That's not a problem."

"But it is. They won't let me out of the country without—'

"You only need a passport to get back into the States. And, of course, to enter Quidar." He tugged gently on her hand and drew her close to his side. "You forget, sweetheart. You're traveling with me. I'll see to it you'll have no difficulty reentering your country." His smile tilted. "And I can guarantee you'll be allowed to enter mine."

"But..."

She hesitated, trying to find the right words. His explanation was simple. What wasn't simple was the sudden panic she felt at the thought of leaving everything familiar and going into the unknown with a man she hardly knew.

Without a passport, she'd be totally dependent on Nick. And she knew what that kind of dependency could do to a woman after seeing the mistakes of her mother's two marriages and experiencing the problems of her own.

"I'd just feel better if I had my passport." She tried to soften the words with a smile. "It would seem strange to travel abroad without—"

The phone beside Nick buzzed. He picked it up.

"Yes?" he said brusquely, and then he frowned. "Please tell my father I'm on my way. No, no, I'm glad you called.

Yes. I understand.'' He put the phone down slowly, his face troubled.

''Nick? What is it?''

A muscle knotted in his cheek, a sign she'd come to know meant he was worried.

''That was my father's physician. My father hasn't been well. And now this added stress...'' He fell silent, then cleared his throat. ''Well,'' he said briskly, ''what were we talking about?''

Amanda twined her fingers through his. ''You were explaining why I didn't need my passport.''

''And you were explaining why you did.''

''Well, I was wrong.'' She brought his hand to her face and pressed it to her cheek. ''Ah, the joys of traveling with the Lion of the Desert,'' she said lightly.

Nick looked deep into her eyes. ''I'm not the Lion of the Desert when I'm with you,'' he said, and he drew her into his arms and kissed her.

They changed planes in Dallas and settled into the first-class cabin of the commercial flight that would take them to Quidar.

The flight attendant who brought them champagne recognized Nick and dropped a quick curtsy. ''Your Highness. How nice to have you with us again.''

She turned brightly curious eyes on Amanda. Nick took her hand.

''Thank you,'' he said politely, and asked something inconsequential about the projected flight.

''Forgive me for not introducing you,'' he said softly when they were alone again.

''That's all right.'' It wasn't. Amanda knew how stiff her words must sound. ''You're under no obligation to—''

''Sweetheart.'' Nick leaned close and brushed his lips over hers. ''I'm only protecting you from reading about yourself in tomorrow's papers.''

''Are you serious?''

''Deadly serious. I've no reason to distrust the attendant,

but why take chances? There's a heavy market in celebrity gossip.''

''Yes, but...'' But you're not a celebrity, she'd almost said because she didn't think of him that way. He was a man to her, a man with whom she'd fallen in love, but to the rest of the world, he was the stuff of tabloid headlines. She sighed and rubbed her forehead against his sleeve. ''It must be awful,'' she murmured. ''Never having any privacy, never being able to let down your guard.''

''That's the way it's been most of my life...until now.'' Nick put his hand under Amanda's chin and smiled into her eyes. ''I've let down my guard with you, sweetheart.''

''Have you?'' she said softly.

He nodded. ''I've told you more about myself than I've ever told anyone. And I've never taken anyone with me to Quidar.''

Her heart leaped at what he'd said.

''No one?''

''No one,'' he said solemnly. ''You're the first.'' He leaned closer. ''The first woman I've ever—''

''Dom Pérignon or Taittinger, Your Highness?'' the flight attendant asked cheerfully.

''It doesn't matter,'' Nick said, his eyes locked on Amanda's face. ''What we drink doesn't matter at all.''

They ate dinner, though Amanda was too wound up to do more than pick at hers. What would her first glimpse of Nick's homeland be like? What would his father think about her being with him? What would Nick tell him?

She stole a glance at Nick. He'd opened his omnipresent briefcase and read through some papers. Then he'd reached for the telephone and made several calls, sounding more purposeful, even imperial, with each conversation. He even looked different, his mouth and jaw seemingly set in sterner lines, as if he were changing from the man who'd made such passionate love to her into the man who was the heir to the throne of his country.

Her throat tightened.

''Nick?'' she said as he hit the disconnect button.

He frowned, blinked, stared at her as if, just for a moment, he'd all but forgotten her presence.

"Yes," he said a little impatiently, and then he seemed to give himself a little shake. "Sorry, sweetheart." He put his arm around her, drew her close. "I wanted to take care of some things before we land."

"Have you told your father that you're bringing me with you?"

Nick hesitated. "Yes, I told him."

"And?"

"And what?"

"And what did he say?"

"He said he hoped you were even more beautiful than Scheherazade," Nick said lightly. "I assured him that you were."

"I don't understand."

"There's an ancient legend that says Scheherazade visited Zamidar and the Ivory Palace centuries ago."

Amanda gave him a puzzled smile. "The same Scheherazade who saved her neck by telling that sultan all those stories?"

"The very one." Nick smiled. "Unfortunately, she didn't tell any tall tales when she visited the monarch of Quidar."

She grinned. "Your grandpa, no doubt, a zillion times removed. Well, why didn't she? Tell him stories, I mean."

"There was no reason."

"Ah." Amanda tucked her head against Nick's shoulder. "Nice to know."

"Hmm?"

"That the monarch of Quidar didn't have the power to..." She sliced her hand across her neck and Nick laughed.

"Of course he did."

"He did?"

"Yes." He tipped her chin up and lightly folded his hand around her throat. "He still can," he said softly. "The rulers of my country have always held life-and-death power over those who cross into the kingdom."

"Oh." Her heart skipped a beat. "Does that include the heir to the throne?"

Nick smiled into her eyes, then brushed his mouth over hers. "I can do anything I want with you, once we reach Quidar."

His tone was light, his smile gentle. Still, even though she knew it was foolish, she couldn't help feeling a little uneasy.

"That sounds ominous," she said, and managed a smile in return.

Nick kissed her again. "Come on. Put your head on my shoulder. That's it. Now, love, shut your eyes and get some sleep."

She let him draw her head down, let him gently kiss her eyes closed.

He could do anything he wanted with her, he'd said. And what he wanted was to bring her to the Ivory Palace and call her his love.

They changed planes in Paris, going from the commercial jet to a smaller plane, similar to the one they'd flown to Espada. It, too, bore the emblem of Quidar on the fuselage.

Butterflies were beginning to swarm in Amanda's stomach.

"How much longer until we reach your country?" she asked.

"Just a few hours." Nick took her hand. "Nervous?"

"A little," she admitted.

Why wouldn't she be? She was flying to an unknown place to meet a king. The king was Nick's father, and yes, Nick was a prince—but the Nick she knew was only a man, and her lover.

So long as she kept sight of that, she'd be fine.

The final leg of their journey went quickly. Nick held her hand but spoke to her hardly at all. He seemed—what was the right word? Preoccupied. Even distant. But he would be, considering that all his energies would have to be centered on the problems that had brought him home.

The plane touched down, coasted to a seamless stop. Nick rose to his feet, held out his hand and she took it.

"Ready?" he said softly, and she nodded, even though her heart was pounding, and let him lead her to the exit door.

Blinking, she stepped out into bright sunlight.

All during the past few hours, she'd tried to envision what she'd find at the end of their long journey. She'd conjured up an endless strip of concrete spearing across a barren desert.

What she saw was a small, modern airport, graceful palm trees and, just ahead, the skyline of a small city etched in icy-white relief against a cerulean sky. A line of limousines stood waiting nearby, but she'd lived in New York long enough to have seen strings of big cars before.

The only really startling sight was at their feet, where a dozen men, all wearing desert robes, knelt in obeisance, their foreheads pressed to the concrete runway.

Amanda shot a glance at Nick. His face seemed frozen, as if an ancient, evil wizard had changed him into a stranger.

One of the men stirred. "My Lord Rashid," he said, "we bid you welcome."

"English?" Amanda whispered.

Nick drew her beside him. "English," he said softly, a touch of amusement edging his voice. "The Royal Council usually uses it when addressing me. It's their very polite way of reminding me that I am not truly of Quidar."

"I don't understand."

"You couldn't understand," he said wryly, "without roots that go back three thousand years."

He stepped forward, thanked the council members for the greeting and told them to rise. He didn't mention her or introduce her, but she felt the cold glances of the men, saw their stern expressions.

A shudder raced along her skin.

"You didn't introduce me," she said to Nick as their limousine and the others raced toward the city.

"I will, when the time is right."

"Won't those men wonder who I am?"

"They know you're with me, Amanda. That's sufficient."

The shudder came again but stronger this time.

"Nick?" She took a deep breath, let it out slowly. "Nick, I've been thinking. Maybe...maybe I shouldn't have come with you."

"Don't be ridiculous."

"I mean it. I want to go back."

"No."

"What do you mean, no? I'm telling you—"

"And I said, no."

Amanda swung toward Nick. He was staring straight ahead, arms folded, jaw set.

"Don't speak to me that way," she said carefully. "I don't like it."

Seconds passed. Then he turned toward her, muttered something under his breath and took her in his arms. "Sweetheart, forgive me. I have a lot on my mind. Of course you can leave if that's what you really want. I'm hoping it isn't. I want you here, with me."

"I want to be with you, too. It's just that...I think—"

Nick stopped her with a kiss. "Remember what I once told you? Stop thinking."

She knew he was teasing, but the throwaway remark still angered her. "Dammit," she said, pushing free of his arms, "that is such a miserably chauvinistic—"

"Okay. So I'm a chauvinist." Nick put his hand under her chin and gently turned her face away from him. "Chew me out later, but for now, wouldn't you like to take a look at the Ivory Palace?"

"No," she said tersely. "I'm not the least bit..."

Oh, but she was.

The Ivory Palace rose from the dusty white city of Zamidar like a fairy-tale castle. Ornate, brightly polished gates swung slowly open, admitting them to a cobblestone courtyard. Flowers bloomed everywhere, their colorful heads nodding gently in a light breeze. Beyond the palace, jagged mountain peaks soared toward the sky.

Their limousine stopped at the foot of a flight of marble steps. Amanda reached for Nick's hand as a servant opened the door, then all but fell to the ground as they stepped from the car. Nick didn't give any sign that he'd noticed. He didn't seem to notice the servants who lined the steps as they mounted them, either, even though each one bowed to him.

It was, Amanda thought dazedly, like being passed from link to link along a human chain that led, at last, into the vast entry hall of the palace itself, where Abdul, shiny black suit and all, waited to greet them.

Until that moment, she hadn't realized how good it would be to see a familiar face.

"Abdul," she said, holding out her hand, "how nice to—"

"My lord," the old man said, and bowed. "Welcome home."

"Thank you, Abdul. Is my father here?"

"Your father has been called away from the palace. He says to tell you he is happy you have returned and that he will dine with you this evening. I trust you had a pleasant journey."

"Pleasant but tiring." Nick gathered Amanda close to his side. "Ms. Benning and I will want to rest."

"Everything is in readiness, sire."

"You will call me when you know my father is en route."

"Of course, Lord Rashid. May I get you something to eat?"

"Not now, thank you. Just have a tray sent to my quarters in an hour or so."

"Certainly, my lord."

Abdul bowed. Nick stepped past him and led Amanda through the hall, past walls of pink-veined marble and closed doors trimmed with gold leaf, to a massive staircase. Halfway to the second floor, she peered over her shoulder.

"Nick?"

"Hmm?"

"He's still bent in half."

"Who?"

"Abdul. Aren't you going to tell him to stand up?"

"No."

"For heaven's sake—"

Nick's arm tightened around her. "Keep walking."

"Yes, but—"

"There is no 'yes, but.' This is Quidar. Things are different here. The customs—"

"Damn your customs! That old man—"

She gasped as Nick swung her into his arms, strode down the hall, elbowed open the door to one of the rooms, stepped inside and kicked it shut.

"Watch what you say to me, woman," he growled, and dumped her on her feet.

"No, *you* watch what you say to me!" Amanda slapped her hands on her hips. "Who do you think you are, talking to me like that?"

"I'm the Lion of the Desert. And you would do well to remember it."

"My God," she said with a little laugh, "you're serious!"

"Completely serious."

"So much for what you said on the plane. About not being the Lion of the Desert when you're with me."

"My private life isn't the same as my public life," Nick said sharply. "Those customs you think so little of matter a great deal to my people."

"They're antiquated and foolish."

"Perhaps they are, but they're also revered. If I were to tell Abdul not to bow to me, especially on Quidaran soil, he would be humiliated."

"I suppose that's why you left that lineup of slaves standing on their heads outside the palace."

"They're not slaves," Nick said, his voice cold. "They're servants."

"And you like having servants."

"Dammit!" He marched away, turned and marched back. "It's an honor to serve in the royal household."

Amanda gave a derisive snort.

"You might not understand that, but it's true. And yes, that's exactly why I didn't stop them from bowing to me. Only my father, the members of his council and, someday, the woman I take as my wife, will not have to bow to me."

"I'm sure that will thrill her."

Nick grabbed Amanda's arms, yanked her against him and kissed her.

"You can't solve every problem that way," she gasped, twisting her face from his, but he caught hold of her chin, brought her mouth to his and kissed her again and again until her lips softened and clung to his.

"I don't want to talk about Quidar," he said softly, "or its rules and customs. Not right now."

"But we have to—"

"We don't," he murmured, and slipped his tongue between her lips.

She moaned, lifted her hands and curled them into his shirt. "Nick—"

"Amanda." He smiled and kissed her throat.

"Nick, stop that. I'm serious."

"So am I. I'm seriously interested in knowing which you'd rather do—debate the historical and social validity of Quidaran culture or take a bath with Quidar's heir to the throne."

She drew back in his encircling arms and tried to scowl, but Nick's eyes glinted with laughter and, after a few seconds, she couldn't help laughing, too.

"You're impossible, O Lion of the Desert."

"On the contrary, Ms. Benning. I'm just a man who believes in cleanliness."

She laughed again, but her laughter faded as he began unbuttoning her blouse.

"What are you doing?" she said with a catch in her voice.

"I'm doing what I've ached to do for hours," he whispered. Slowly, his eyes never leaving hers, he undressed her. Then he stepped back and looked at her, his gaze as hot as a caress. "My beautiful Amanda." He reached for her, gathered her against him until she could feel the race of his heart against hers. "Tell me what you want," he said as he had done once before, and she moaned and showed him with her mouth, her hands, her heart.

Nick lifted her into his arms and carried her into an enormous bathroom, to a sunken marble tub the size of a small swimming pool. Water spilled into the tub from a winged gold swan; perfume-scented steam drifted into the air like wisps of fog.

Amanda sighed as he stepped down into the tub with her still in his arms. "Mmm. Someone's already run our bath. How nice."

"Uh-huh." Nick lowered her gently to her feet, linked his hands at the base of her spine. "Another little benefit you get when you're known as a lion."

She laughed softly and stroked her hands down his chest. "Lions are pussycats in disguise."

Nick caught his breath as she curled her fingers around him. "I've always liked cats," he said thickly. He drew her against him with one arm, slipped his hand between her thighs. "I like to hear them purr when I stroke their silken fur."

Amanda caught her breath. "Nick. Oh, Nick..."

He stepped back, sat on the edge of the tub, then drew her between his legs. "Your breasts are so beautiful," he whispered, and bent his head to taste them. "I could feast on them forever."

I could love you forever, she thought. I could be yours, Nicholas al Rashid. I could—

He clasped her hips, drew her to him. "Come to me, sweetheart," he said softly.

She put her hands on his shoulders. Then, slowly, she lowered herself on him, impaled herself on him, took him deep into her silken softness until his velvet heat filled her. Nick groaned, lifted her legs, wrapped them around his waist.

"Amanda." He cupped her face in his hand, kissed her deeply. "My beloved."

My beloved. The words had the sweetness, the softness, of a promise. Her heart filled with joy.

"You'll be mine forever," he said quietly. "I'll never let you leave me."

"I'll never want to leave you," she said in a broken whis-

per, and then he moved, moved again until she was clinging
to his shoulders and sobbing his name.

She collapsed in his arms as he drove into her one last time.
They stayed that way, she with her face buried against him,
he with his arms tightly around her. At last he stirred. He
kissed her mouth, her breasts, swung her into his arms, carried
her to his bed and held her until she drifted into exhausted
sleep.

When she awoke, night held the room in moonlit darkness.
She was alone in the bed; Nick was gone and she smiled,
imagining him talking with his father, telling him what he had
told her, that he loved her, that she would be with him forever.

Tonight, she thought, tonight she would say the words.

"I love you, Nicholas al Rashid," she whispered into the
silence. "I love you with all my heart."

A knock sounded at the door.

"Nick?" she said happily. But Nick wouldn't be so formal.
Ah. Of course. He'd told Abdul to have a tray sent to his
rooms. "Just a minute."

She reached for the lamp on the table beside the bed and
switched it on. What was protocol in such a situation? She
had no robe. Would it be all right to stay where she was,
wrapped in the silk sheet like a mummy? Was that the custom
for the woman who was the beloved of the Lion of the Desert?
The woman who would spend her life with—

The door swung open. Amanda grabbed the sheet and
dragged it up to her chin. "Excuse me. I didn't...Abdul?"

The little man stood in the doorway, but he didn't look quite
so little now. He stood straight, arms folded, a look of disdain
on his face. Two robed figures flanked him—two tall, mus-
cular figures whose stance mimicked his.

A whisper of fear sighed along Amanda's skin, but she
spoke with cool authority. "Is it the custom to enter a bedroom
before you're given permission?"

"You are to come with me, Ms. Benning."

"Come where? Has Lord Rashid sent for me?"

"I act on his command."

That wasn't the answer to her question. Amanda licked her lips. "Where is he? Where is the prince?"

The old man jerked his head and the robed figures advanced toward the bed.

"Dammit, Abdul! Did you hear what I said? When I tell Lord Rashid about this—"

"Lord Rashid has given orders that you are to be moved to different quarters. It is your choice if you come willingly or if you do not."

Amanda's heart banged into her throat. "Moved?"

"That is correct."

"But where—where am I to be moved?"

The old man smiled. She had never seen him smile before.

"To the harem, Ms. Benning, where you will be kept in readiness for the pleasure of the Lion of the Desert for so long as he may wish it."

CHAPTER TWELVE

AMANDA shrieked like a wild woman.

She cursed and kicked, and was rewarded by a grunt when her foot connected with a groin, but she was no match for the two burly men.

They subdued her easily, wrapped her in the sheet and carried her through the palace as if she were an oversize package, one man supporting her knees, the other holding her shoulders. Abdul headed the little procession up stairs and down, through endless corridors.

She kept screaming and kicking, but it did no good.

Her captors ignored her, and though they passed other people in the halls, nobody took notice. Nobody cared. As frightened as she'd been when Abdul's henchmen grabbed her, that was the most terrifying realization of all.

Finally, the men came to a stop before a massive door. Abdul snapped out an order, the door groaned open, and Amanda's captors stepped across the threshold and dumped her, unceremoniously, on the floor.

Abdul clapped his hands and the men backed from the room. The door swung shut. Amanda, shaking as much with rage as fear, kicked free of the sheet and sat up. She looked at Abdul, standing over her. He'd traded his shiny black suit for a long, heavily embroidered robe; his face was expressionless.

"You horrible old man!" Panting, weeping, she struggled to her feet, clutching the sheet around her. "You'll rot in hell for this, Abdul, do you hear me? When I tell the sheikh what you've done to me..."

"I have done nothing to you, Ms. Benning. My orders to

159

my men were very clear. They were not to hurt you, and they have not.''

"They trussed me up like a—a Christmas gift!"

An evil smile creased Abdul's leathery face. "More like a birthday gift, I think."

"What's that supposed to mean?"

"All will be explained in due time."

"Listen, you miserable son of a—"

"Women do not use obscenities in Quidar," the old man said sharply. "It is against our rules and customs."

"Oh, no. No, that's not the custom. Brutalizing women. Kidnapping them. *That's* the custom." She hung on to the sheet with one hand and pointed a trembling finger at Abdul. "You're finished. I just hope you know that. When Lord Rashid hears what you've done—"

"There is food and drink in the next room, and clothing, as well."

"I don't care what's in the next room!"

"That is your prerogative," Abdul said calmly. "At any rate, Lord Rashid will be with you shortly."

"You mean Lord Rashid will be with *you,* you bastard! And when he does, he'll have your head."

Abdul laughed. First a smile, now a laugh? Amanda knew that wasn't good. She was more frightened than ever, but she'd have died rather than let the old bastard know it, so she drew herself up and glared at him.

"What's so funny?"

"You are, Ms. Benning. You see, it was Lord Rashid who instructed me to have you brought here."

"Don't be ridiculous. Nick would never…"

Abdul turned his back to her, walked to the door and opened it. Amanda made a leap for it, but the door swung shut with a thud. She heard the lock click as the bolt slid home, but she grabbed the knob anyway, pulled, tugged…

The door didn't move.

For a moment, for a lifetime, she stood absolutely still, not moving, not blinking, not even breathing.

"No," she finally whispered, "no..."

Her voice rose to a terrified wail. She fell against the door, pounded it with her fists. The sheet she'd wrapped around herself fell, forgotten, to the floor.

"Abdul," she shouted, "old man, you can't do this!"

But he could. The silence on the other side of the door was confirmation of that. Her screams faded to sobs of despair. She gave the door one last jarring blow, then slid to the carpet.

God, what was happening? What was Abdul up to? What had he meant when he said Nick had told him to bring her here? It wasn't true. It couldn't be. And that nonsense about taking her to the harem. Harems didn't exist anymore, except in bad movies.

Okay. She had to calm down instead of panicking. Abdul had done this to frighten her, but she wouldn't let that happen. She'd take deep breaths. Slow and easy. Breathe in, breathe out. Good. She could feel her pulse rate slowing. It was only a matter of time before Nick realized she was missing. He'd come looking for her. He'd find her—

"Ms. Benning?"

Amanda jerked her head up. A dark-haired woman stood over her, holding a pale green caftan over her arm.

"Would you like to put this on, Ms. Benning? Or would you prefer to choose something for yourself?"

"Thank God!" Amanda clutched at the sheet and shot to her feet. "Look, there's been some horrible mistake. You have to get word to Nick—to Lord Rashid—"

"My name is Sara."

Her name was Sara? Who cared about her name?

"Sara. Sara, you must find the sheikh and tell him—"

"Let me help you with this," Sara said pleasantly. "Just let go of that...what is that anyway?" She gave Amanda a little smile. "It looks like a sheet."

"It *is* a sheet! Two men came into my room—into Lord Rashid's quarters—and—"

"Raise your arms, Ms. Benning. Now let me pull this over your head. That's it. Oh, yes. The pale green is perfect for you." Sara smoothed her hand over Amanda's hair. "Such a lovely color," she said, "but so short. Well, it will grow out, and when it does, I'll plait it with flowers. Or perhaps Lord Rashid would prefer emeralds—"

Amanda slapped the woman's hand away. "I'm not a doll! And I'm not going to be here long enough for you to plait my hair with anything."

"I'm sure you will, Ms. Benning," Sara said soothingly. "A favorite may be kept for months. Years, perhaps."

"Dammit, I've no intention of becoming a 'favorite'. If you know what's good for you, you'll find Lord Rashid and tell him—"

"Tell him what, Amanda?"

Amanda spun around. Nick stood in the doorway.

"Nick! Oh, thank God you've…"

Her words trailed to silence. It *was* Nick, wasn't it? He looked so different. No jeans, no T-shirt. No carefully tailored suit and tie. Instead, he wore a flowing white robe trimmed in gold. He looked exactly as he'd looked in the *Gossip* photo. Tall. Proud. Magnificently masculine…

And heart-stoppingly dangerous.

He looked past her to Sara, who had dropped to the floor at the sound of his voice. "Leave us," he said brusquely.

Sara scrambled to her feet and backed quickly from the room.

Nick shut the door and folded his arms. "Well? What did you wish Sara to tell me?"

"Why—why, about this. About what Abdul did to me…"

Amanda fell silent. He was looking at her so strangely. She wanted his arms around her, his heart beating against hers. She wanted him to hold her close and tell her that this was all a terrible mistake or a bad joke gone wrong. She wanted anything but for him to stand as he was, unmoving, a stranger with a stern face and cold eyes.

"Nick?" Her voice was a dry whisper. "Nick, what's going on?"

Nick almost laughed. This woman who had slept with him,

who had stolen his heart and sold its contents to the world, wanted to know what was going on. She said it with such innocence, too—but then, why wouldn't she?

She had no way of knowing that Abdul, with his usual efficiency, had managed to get a copy of the lead article in next week's *Gossip* and that he'd brought it to Nick, trembling as he did, wringing his hands and whispering, "Lord Rashid, the American woman has betrayed you."

"I had you moved to new quarters," Nick said with a tight smile. "Don't you like them? This is the oldest part of the Ivory Palace. I thought it would appeal to you, considering your supposed interest in interior design." He eased away from the door, strolled around the room, pausing at an intricately carved chair, then at a table inlaid with tiny blocks of colored woods. "These things are very old and valuable. There's great interest in them at Christie's, but I've no wish to sell—"

"Dammit!" Amanda strode after him, hands clenched, her terror rapidly giving way to anger. "I'm not interested in tables and chairs."

"No. You most certainly are not."

He'd tossed the words out like a barb, but she decided to ignore them. What she wanted were answers, and she wanted them fast.

"I want to know why you had me brought here. Why you let Abdul and his—his goons wrap me up like laundry, dump me in a heap and lock the door!"

Nick turned toward her. "They brought you here because it is the custom."

"The custom. Well, damn the custom! If I hear that word one more time…" She took a breath and reminded herself to stay calm. "What custom?"

"The Quidaran custom, of course."

God, he was infuriating. That insulting little smile. That I'm-so-clever glint in his eyes. Staying calm wasn't going to be easy.

"Everything is a Quidaran custom," she said coldly. "But if abusing women falls into that category, I'm out of here."

Nick's brows lifted. "No one has abused you, Amanda."

"No? Well, what do you call it, then? Your thugs burst into my room, dragged me out of my bed—"

"It is *my* room," he said softly. "And my bed."

"I know that. I only meant—"

"And I no longer wanted you in either one."

His words skewered her heart and put a stop to the anger raging through her.

"But you said..." Her voice trembled. She stopped and took a deep breath. "You said you wanted me to be yours forever."

Yes. Oh, yes, he thought, he had. The memory was almost more painful than he could bear. He knew it would be years— a lifetime—before he managed to put it aside.

What a fool he'd been to want her. To call her his beloved. To have told his father he'd found the missing half of his heart, the part of himself each man searches for, without knowing it, from the moment he first draws breath....

"Nick." Her voice was filled with pleading. "Nick, please, tell me this is all some awful joke."

"Did I say I wanted you with me forever?" He smiled coolly, lifted his shoulders in an expressive shrug. "It was a figure of speech."

Amanda stared at him. "A figure of speech?"

"Of course." Nick forced a smile to his lips. "'Forever' is a poetic concept." He walked slowly toward her, still smiling, and stopped when they were only inches apart. "Don't look so worried," he said softly. "It won't be forever, but it will be a long time before I tire of you."

"Please," she said shakily, "stop this. You're scaring me. I don't—I don't know what you're talking about."

Slowly, he wrapped his hand around the nape of her neck and tugged her to him. She stumbled, put out her hands and laid them against his chest.

"Don't you?"

"No. I don't understand why you had me brought here. I don't even know where I am. The oldest part of the palace, you said."

"Indeed." Nick's eyes dropped to her mouth. Her sweet, beautiful, lying mouth. "I had you brought here because it's where you belong." His gaze lifted, caught hers. "You were my birthday present, darling. Remember?"

She stared at him. "A birthday...? But that was just a joke. You misunderstood what Dawn meant—"

"Nonsense."

"It's not nonsense. I explained everything. That I was a designer. That Dawn only wanted me to do your apartment."

Nick laughed softly. "You're a designer all right. Your 'design' was to worm your way into my life." He reached out a finger, traced the outline of her mouth with its tip. "What you are is a man's dream come true. And now you're right where you belong." His smile was slow and sexy. "Welcome to the harem, Amanda."

She jerked back as if the touch of his hand had scorched her. "What?"

Nick smiled, bent his head, brushed his mouth over hers. She didn't move, didn't respond, didn't so much as breathe.

"Didn't Abdul tell you?"

"He said something about a harem, yes. But I thought..."

His hand cupped her throat, his thumb seeming to measure the fluttering race of her pulse.

"You don't... Harems don't exist," she said quickly. "Not anymore. That's all changed."

"This is the kingdom of Quidar. Nothing changes here unless the king—or his heir—wishes it."

"Do you really expect me to believe you—you have a harem? A bunch of women you keep as—as sexual slaves?" She gave a weak laugh. "Honestly, Nick—"

"Do you recall what I told you about your use of that word, 'slaves'?" Nick cupped her shoulders, drew her stiff body to his. "I assure you, it's an honor to warm my bed."

"This isn't funny, dammit. Surely you can't think I'd—"

She gasped as his mouth covered hers in a long, drugging kiss.

"I must admit, I found you enjoyable," he said calmly, when he finally lifted his head and looked into her eyes. "You have a beautiful body. A lovely face. And you've proven an apt pupil in the ways to pleasure a man."

Her face whitened. She tried to pull free of him, but his hands dug into her flesh.

"So, I've decided to keep you. For a while, at any rate." She cried out as he thrust his hand into her hair and tugged her head back so that her face was raised to his. "Don't look so shocked, darling. You'll enjoy it, I promise. And think of the excellent material you'll have to sell when I finally tire of you and send you home."

"Sell? What 'material'? What are you—"

"Damn you!" Nick's smile vanished. "Don't pull that wide-eyed look on me! You were too impetuous. If only you'd waited...but I suppose you thought you'd be back in New York, safe and sound, before the next issue of that rag hit the streets."

"What rag? I have no idea what—"

"'My Days and Nights with Nicholas al Rashid'," Nick said coldly. He thrust her from him hard enough so she stumbled. "Such a trite title, Amanda. Or does *Gossip* write its own headlines?"

Amanda stared at him in disbelief. "What has *Gossip* to do with this?"

Nick's mouth thinned. He reached inside his robe, took out a sheet of paper and shoved it at her. She gave it a bewildered glance.

"What is this?"

"Take it," he said grimly. "Go on."

She looked down at the paper he'd pushed into her hand. It was a copy of what appeared to be an article bylined, "Special to *Gossip*, from Amanda Benning."

"'My Days and Nights with...'" she read in a shaky whisper. Her face paled, and she looked up. "Nick, for God's sake, this is a hoax. Surely you don't think I'd write something like this.''

"Read it."

His voice flicked over her like a whip. Amanda looked at the paper and moistened her lips. "'My Days and Nights with...'" Color rushed into her face. "'With the sexy sheikh...'" She looked at him again. "Whoever wrote this is talking about—about—"

"About what it's like to make love to..." Nick's jaw tightened. "What was the phrase? Ah, yes. I remember now. "To 'an elegant, exciting savage'.'' His mouth twisted. "I've been called a lot of things, Ms. Benning, but never that."

"Nick. Listen to me. I'd never do this. Never! How could you even think...? Someone else did it. Wrote this—this thing and used my—"

"Read the final paragraph," he commanded. "Aloud."

She drew a shaky breath. "'As it turns out, the Lion of the Desert is...'" She stopped and lifted imploring eyes to his. "No," she whispered. "Nick, I can't—"

"'As it turns out,'" he said coldly, calling up the ugly words that had been forever burned into his brain, "'the Lion of the Desert is more than a stud. He also has a talent for three-card monte. The sexy sheikh has a souvenir from that time, a two-headed coin that's a reminder of the days when he hustled his school chums...'" Nick looked directly into Amanda's eyes. "I never told that story to anyone," he said softly. "Not to anyone but you."

"And you think..." The paper fell from her hand. She reached out to Nick, her fingers curling into his sleeve. "I swear to you, I didn't write this!"

"Perhaps you didn't hear me. No one knows about that coin except you."

"Someone knows. Someone wrote this, put my name on it. Don't you see? This is a lie. I'd never—"

She cried out as he grabbed the neckline of the silk caftan and tore it from the hollow of her throat to the hem. She tried to tug the edges together, but Nick captured her hands. "Don't play the terrified virgin with me. Not when you've shared the intimate details of my life with millions of strangers.''

"Nick. I beg you—''

"Go on. Beg me. I want you to beg me!'' He dragged her into his arms, clamped her against him, caught her face in his hands and forced it to his. "So, I'm a savage, am I?'' His teeth showed in a quick, feral grin. "That's fine. I think I'm going to enjoy living down to that description.''

"Don't. Nick, don't do this. I love you. I love—''

He kissed her, hard, his mouth covering hers with barely suppressed rage, his teeth and tongue savaging her while his fingers dug into her jaw.

"Don't speak to me of love, you bitch!''

He kissed her again and again, deaf to her pleas, unmoved by her desperate struggles, lifted her into his arms, tumbled her onto a pile of silk cushions and straddled her.

"Speak to me of what you know. Of betrayal. Of mindless sex. Of how it feels to be a whore.''

The sound of her hand cracking against his cheek echoed through the room like a gunshot. Nick's head jerked back; he raised his hand in retaliation.

"Go on,'' Amanda said. Her voice trembled, but her gaze was steady. "Hit me. Dishonor me. Do whatever you came here to do because you couldn't possibly hurt me any more than you already have.''

Nick stared down at her while the seconds slipped away. God, he thought, oh, God, how close she'd come to turning him into the savage she'd called him. He cursed, shot to his feet, grabbed Amanda's wrist and dragged her after him.

"Abdul!'' he shouted as he flung the door open.

The little man stepped forward. "Yes, my lord?''

"Bring the woman her clothes.''

"But, sire...''

Nick shoved Amanda into the corridor. "She will dress and you will take her to the airport. See to it she's flown to Paris and put on the next plane for New York.''

Abdul bowed low. "As you wish, Lord Rashid.''

"Get her out of my sight!" Nick's voice shook with rage and the pain of betrayal. "Get her out of my sight," he whispered again, once he was back in his own rooms with the door closed and locked.

Then he sank onto the bed, the bed where he'd finally admitted that he'd fallen in love with Amanda Benning, buried his face in his hands and did something no Lion of the Desert had ever done in all the centuries before him.

Nicholas al Rashid, Lord of the Realm and Sublime Heir to the Imperial Throne of Quidar, wept.

An hour later, Abdul knocked on the door. "Lord Rashid?"

Nick stirred. He'd changed back into jeans—the truth was, he always felt like a fool in that silly white-and-gold robe. He was even feeling a little better.

After all, he'd get over this. Amanda was only a woman, and the world was filled with women....

"Lord Rashid? May I come in?"

It had been his mistake, that he'd opened his heart. He should have known better. Everyone always wanted something from him. The instant celebrity of being seen in his company. The right to mention his name in seemingly casual conversation. The supposed status that came of saying he was a friend or, at least, an acquaintance.

That was just the way things were. He knew it; he'd known it all his adult life. Why should he have expected things to be different with Amanda?

Why should he have let himself think, even for a moment, that she loved him for himself, not for who he was or what he might do for her?

The knock sounded again, more forcefully. "Sire. It is I. Abdul."

Nick sighed, switched on a lamp and went slowly to the door. "Yes?" he said as he pulled it open. "What is it?"

Abdul knelt down and touched his forehead to the floor. "I thought you would wish to know that it is done, my lord. The woman is gone."

"Thank you."

"You need trouble yourself with thoughts of her no longer."

"Did she...?" Nick cleared his throat. "Did she say anything more?"

"Sire?"

"Did she send any message for me?"

"Only more lies, my lord."

"More lies..."

"Yes. That she had not done this thing."

Nick nodded. "Yes. Of course. She'll deny it to the end." He looked down at the old man, still doubled over with his forehead pressed to the tile. "Abdul. Please, stand up."

"I cannot, sire. It is not the custom."

"The custom," Nick said irritably. "The custom be damned!" He grabbed the old man's arm and hoisted him to his feet. "You're too old for this nonsense, Abdul. Besides, it's time for some changes in this place."

"I think not, my lord. Your father would wish—"

"My father agrees."

"About change?" Abdul laughed politely. "That cannot be, sire. Your father understands the importance of things continuing as they always have. He may not have understood it once, but—"

"What's that supposed to mean?"

Abdul bit his lip. "Nothing, sire. Just—just the meandering thoughts of an old man."

"Well, prepare yourself for some upsets, Abdul." Nick crossed the room and switched on another light. "My father is going to abdicate the throne."

"Already? I assumed he would wait until he was much older, but that is good, sire. Putting the kingdom in your hands while you are still young is—"

"He's not abdicating for me."

The old man paled. "They why would he abdicate?"

"It's time Quidar entered the twenty-first century. There

will be elections. The people will choose a council. There'll be no more bowing and scraping, no more—''

"That woman. May her wretched soul burn in hell!"

Nick turned around, his head cocked. "What?"

"Nothing, sire. I, ah, I'll go and arrange for your meal to be served. You must be hungry—"

"Are you referring to Ms. Benning?"

The old man hesitated, then nodded. "I am, my lord. There is no reason not to admit it now. She was not good for you."

"What is good or not good for me is my affair," Nick said sharply.

"Of course. I only meant—"

"Yes. I know." Nick sighed and raked his fingers through his hair. "It doesn't matter. She's gone. And you're right. She wasn't good for me."

"Indeed, she was not. A woman who would pretend illness just to gain access to your study—"

"Access to my...?"

"The night of your birthday party, my lord." Abdul snorted. "Such a lie, that she had a headache."

Nick looked at the old man. "How did you know she had a headache?" he asked softly.

Abdul hesitated. "Well, I—I... You rang for aspirin, sire."

"I rang for coffee."

"Ah, yes. Of course. I meant that. You rang for coffee, and then you told her the story of the two-headed coin." Abdul clamped his lips together.

Nick's eyes narrowed. "You were listening," he said. "At the door."

"No. Certainly not."

"You were listening," Nick repeated grimly. "Otherwise, how would you know I'd told her about the coin?"

"I, ah, I must have..." A fine sheen of sweat moistened Abdul's forehead.

"Must have what?" Nick walked slowly toward his secretary. "How could you know I told her about the coin that night?"

The old man dropped to his knees and grasped the cuff of Nick's jeans in his fingers. "I did it for you," he whispered. "For you, and for Quidar."

"Did what?" Nick reached down, grabbed Abdul by the shoulder and hauled him to his feet. "Damn you, what did you do for me and for Quidar?"

"She was wrong for you, sire. As wrong as your mother had been for your father. Foreign women know nothing of our ways."

"Tell me what you did," Nick said through gritted teeth, "or so help me, Abdul…"

"I did my duty."

"Your duty," Nick said softly.

Abdul nodded.

"How did you 'do your duty', old man?"

"Miss Burgess called while you were in Texas with Ms. Benning. She was angry."

"Go on."

"She said—she said to give you a message, sire. She was writing a piece for *Gossip* that would teach you that you couldn't make a fool of her."

Nick let go of Abdul. He clenched his fists and jammed his hands into the back pockets of his jeans. He knew that was the only way he could keep from wrapping them around the old man's scrawny throat.

"And?" he said carefully.

"I offered money for her silence. She laughed and said there wasn't enough money in the world to keep her quiet. Oh, I paced the floor for hours, sire, searching for a solution, but I could think of none."

"And you didn't think to call me?"

"I didn't wish to upset you, my lord." Abdul clasped his hands together in supplication. "I wished to help you, sire, and to help Quidar. If I couldn't stop the Burgess woman from writing the *Gossip* article, I would use it, just as I'd used that picture of you and her on the beach."

Nick stared at Abdul. "Are you telling me that you sold that photo to *Gossip*?"

"I did not 'sell' it, Lord Rashid. I would never..." Abdul took a quick step back. "Sire, don't you understand? I could see what you could not. These foreign devils, tormenting you—"

"What the hell are you talking about?"

"The Benning woman was the worst. She was a temptress. A succubus. And you were falling under her spell."

"For the love of God!" Nick barked out a laugh and raked his hand through his hair. "This isn't the Dark Ages, man. I wasn't succumbing to a spell. I was falling in love!"

Abdul stood as straight as Nick had ever seen him. "The Lion of the Desert must marry a woman who understands our ways."

"The Lion of the Desert must try damned hard not to slam you against the wall," Nick growled. "Go on. What did you do next?"

"I telephoned Miss Burgess. I suggested we could help each other."

"Meaning?"

"I..." For the first time, the old man hesitated. "I gave her some information. I said she might consider using it, along with a different identity." He made a strangled sound as Nick grabbed him by the neck and hoisted him to his toes. "Lord Rashid." Abdul clawed at the powerful hand around his throat. "Sire, I cannot breathe."

Nick let go. The old man collapsed on the floor like a bundle of dirty clothes.

"You son of a bitch," Nick whispered. "You told Deanna about that coin."

"For the good of Quidar, sire," Abdul gasped. "It hurt no one. Surely you can see that. A simple tale about a coin—"

"A simple tale that I thought proved I'd been betrayed by the woman I love."

Nick swung away from the huddled form at his feet and

strode toward the door. Abdul pulled himself up and hurried after him.

"Lord Rashid? Where are you going?"

"To Paris," Nick said. "To New York. To the ends of the earth, until I find Amanda." He looked at Abdul; the old man cowered under that icy gaze and fell to his knees. "And you'd better not be within the borders of this kingdom when I return," he said softly, "or I'll revive one old custom and have your neck on a chopping block."

"Sire. Oh, sire, I beg you. Don't banish me. Please…"

Nick slammed the door. Half an hour later, he was on a jet, hurtling through the night sky toward Paris.

CHAPTER THIRTEEN

WEARY travelers sprawled across the seats in the departure lounge at Paris's Charles de Gaulle Airport.

Their New York–bound plane was still on the ground, its takeoff already delayed by more than three hours. The mechanics had yet to solve a perplexing electrical problem. Until they did, the passengers wouldn't be going anywhere. There was no substitute plan available, so they'd just have to wait it out.

Waiting was the last thing Amanda felt like doing. She knew it was childish but all she wanted was to get home, not just to the States and New York but to her own apartment, where things were familiar and real. Maybe then she could erase the past few days from her head and heart, and start putting things into their proper perspective.

"I just don't understand it!" a querulous voice said.

Amanda turned toward the gray-haired matron who'd dropped into the seat next to hers. "Sorry?"

"The airline," the woman said. "The lie it keeps feeding us. Just look at that airplane out there. Anyone can see there's nothing wrong with it. Why would they expect us to believe an electrical problem is the reason for this awful delay?"

"I'm sure that's what it is," Amanda said politely.

"Nonsense. Electricity is electricity. That's what I told the man at the desk. 'Whom do you think you're fooling?' I said. 'Just put in a new fuse.' And he said…"

The woman's voice droned on. After a while, Amanda closed the magazine she'd been pretending to read and rose to her feet. "Excuse me," she said, and walked to a seat at the far end of the waiting area.

There was no point in trying to change the woman's mind.

If there was one thing the past few days had taught her, it was that people would always believe what they wanted to believe, no matter what anyone told them.

Nick had wanted to believe the very worst about her, that she'd tell the entire world about him, about their most intimate secrets—

"Hi."

She blinked, looked up. A man was standing over her. He was good-looking. Handsome, actually. He had a nice smile and a great face—but that was all he had, all he'd ever have, because he wasn't Nick.

"Miserable, huh? This long delay, I mean—"

"Excuse me," Amanda said for the second time.

She stood up, tucked her hands into the pockets of her jacket and walked out of the waiting area toward the end of the terminal where there were lots of empty seats. The lights were turned low. That was fine. She was in the mood for shadows and darkness.

The man she'd cut dead probably thought she was rude or crazy or maybe both. Well, what was she supposed to have said?

Look, this is a waste of time. I'm not interested in men just now. Or maybe she should have explained that she was too busy thinking about another man to manage even small talk with a stranger.

Oh, hell.

There was no point in thinking about Nick. She'd done nothing except think about him and the humiliation he'd heaped on her. That was all he'd done ever since Abdul had marched her out of the Ivory Palace.

Somewhere along the way, self-doubt had taken the place of anger. What would have happened if only she'd said this thing or that; if she'd somehow forced Nick to listen to her. And then, finally, she'd faced the truth.

Torturing herself wouldn't change a thing. Nick would believe what he wanted to believe no matter what she said. It wasn't as if she'd let some chance to make him see the truth slip through her fingers.

The only mistake she'd made was to have gotten involved with him in the first place.

End of story.

Their affair, their relationship, whatever you wanted to call it, was over. Feelings changed, things ended, you moved on. Her mother had done that. She had, too.

I'm so riddled with guilt, she'd told Marta after her divorce. *Marriage is supposed to be forever. How will I ever put this behind me?*

And Marta had hugged her and said, *Sweetie, you just do it, that's all. You move on.*

She knew Marta had given her good advice. Excellent advice, really. There was no more logic in agonizing over her failed marriage than there was in wasting time wishing this thing with Nick had never happened or in trying to convince the woman with gray hair that you couldn't fix an airplane's electrical problems by changing a fuse.

You couldn't judge a man's heart by his performance in bed, either.

It was a cold realization but it was honest, and if she'd been fool enough to think Nick's whispered words, his kisses, his caresses, were anything but part of sex, that was her problem.

Amanda sighed, strolled into one of the empty lounges and sank wearily into a chair facing the windows. The jet that would take her home squatted on the tarmac. Mechanics scuttled purposefully around it. Problems were being solved, life was going on, and why wouldn't it?

What had happened with Nick—what she'd been stupid enough to let happen—was nothing but a blip in the overall scheme of things. The planet would go on spinning, the stars would go on shining, everything would be exactly the same.

Certainly they would. She'd be home soon, and Nick would be a distant memory. Thank goodness she'd already figured out that she'd never actually fallen in love with him.

"Mesdames et messieurs..."

The impersonal voice droned from the loudspeaker, first in French, then in English. The flight was still delayed. The airline regretted the inconvenience. Another hour or two, blah, blah, blah.

Amanda stood up and walked closer to the window. The sky was darkening. Was a storm blowing toward them or was night coming on? She couldn't tell anymore. Night and day seemed to have gotten all mixed up, just like her emotions.

Mixed up? That was a laugh. Her emotions had gone crazy. Otherwise, how could she possibly have imagined she loved Nick?

The lengths a woman would go to just to avoid admitting the truth—that she'd succumbed to lust. And lust was what she'd felt for Nicholas al Rashid. Good old garden variety, down-and-dirty lust. Wasn't it pathetic she'd had to tell herself it was love?

This was the twenty-first century. The world had long ago admitted that the female of the species could have the same emotions as her male counterpart. Why should she be any different? One look at the Lion of the Desert and pow, her hormones had gone crazy.

Why wouldn't they? He was gorgeous. It had been as flattering as hell to know he wanted to sleep with her because she'd certainly wanted to sleep with him.

And she had.

Most definitely the end of the story…or it should have been.

The trouble was, no matter how many times she told herself that, the *real* end of the story intruded.

Amanda leaned back against the wall and closed her eyes. The scene played in her mind over and over like a videotape caught in a loop.

Nick, hatred blazing in his silver eyes.

Nick, calling her a whore.

Nick, believing that she'd written that article, that she would ever hurt him or betray him. How could he think it? Didn't he know how much she loved him? That her heart would always long for him, want him, ache for him?

She drew a shaky breath, then slowly let it out.

Okay. So—so maybe she'd loved him just a little. What did it matter? They'd only spent a handful of days together. Surely that didn't really add up to "love."

Love didn't come on with the speed of a hurricane. It didn't overwhelm you. It grew slowly into something deep and everlasting.

And the foolishness of thinking Nick loved her... Oh, it was laughable! He didn't. He never had. He'd called her beloved, said he wanted her with him forever, but so what? She wasn't naive. Men said lots of things they didn't mean in the throes of passion.

Love—real love—wasn't only about sex. It was about little things. Things like taking walks in the rain. Like laughing, maybe even crying, over a movie you've seen before. It was about trust.

Especially trust.

If Nick had loved her, he'd have taken one look at the *Gossip* piece and known it was a fake. "It's a lie," he'd have said if he loved her. And then he'd have set out to discover who'd actually written those horrible things, who'd lied and used her name to drive them apart.

But he hadn't done any of that. He'd turned on her in fury, humiliated her, terrified her, believed she'd violated his confidence, talked about the things they'd done together in bed—

"It was a lie," a husky masculine voice whispered.

Amanda's heart skittered into her throat.

"I know it now, beloved. I only hope you can forgive me for not knowing it then."

The world stood still. Please, she thought, oh, please...

She turned slowly, wanting it to be him, afraid it would be him.

Nick stood in the shadows as still as if he'd been carved from stone.

Her knees buckled. He moved quickly and caught her. "Sweetheart. Oh, sweetheart, what have I done to you?"

His face was inches from hers. She longed to touch his

stubbled jaw, to trace the outline of his mouth with the tip of her finger, but he had broken her heart once and she wasn't about to let him do it again.

"Let go of me, Nick."

He swung her into his arms.

"No," she said breathlessly. "Put me down."

"Hey. Hey!"

Nick turned, still holding Amanda. The man with the nice smile and the great face came toward them.

"What's going on here?"

Nick looked at him. Whatever the man saw in his eyes made him retreat a couple of steps before he spoke up again.

"Say the word, lady, and I'll send this dude packing."

"You'll try," Nick said softly, "But you won't succeed." His arms tightened around Amanda. "This woman belongs to me."

"I don't belong to you! I don't belong to anybody."

His eyes met hers. "Yes, you do." He bent his head and kissed her gently. "You'll always belong to me, and I to you, sweetheart, because we love each other."

The words he'd spoken stunned her. She wanted to tell him she didn't love him, she'd never loved him. She wanted to tell him he'd never loved her—but he smiled into her eyes and she saw something in those cool silver depths that stole her breath away.

"Lady?"

Nick lifted his head. He was smiling, the way he'd smiled after they made love the very first time. "The lady is fine," he said quietly, his eyes never leaving hers.

The man looked from Amanda to Nick and back again. "Yeah," he said with a little laugh, "yeah, I can see that."

Nick set off through the terminal, Amanda still in his arms. She saw the startled faces all around them, the wide eyes of the women, the smiles on the lips of the men. Her cheeks flushed crimson and she buried her face in his shoulder. Doors opened and shut; she felt the rush of cool air against her hot face, the silence of enclosed space.

When she lifted her head and looked up again, they were in Nick's private plane. He let her down slowly. And when her feet touched the floor, her sanity returned.

"What do you think you're doing, Nick?"

He smiled and linked his hands at the base of her spine. "I love you, Amanda."

"Love?" She laughed. "You don't know the meaning of the—"

Nick lifted her face to his and kissed her. She felt her heart turn over, felt the longing to put her arms around him sweep through her blood, but she would not make a fool of herself ever again.

"If you really think you can—you can just pretend what you did never happened..."

Nick put his arm around her, led her into the cockpit.

"What are you doing?"

"Sit down," he said calmly. "And put on your seat belt."

"Don't be ridiculous. I will not—"

He sighed, pushed her gently into the co-pilot's seat and buckled the belt around her.

"Dammit," she sputtered, "you can get away with kidnapping in Quidar, but this is France. You can't just—"

Nick silenced her with a kiss. She moaned; she didn't mean to, but the feel of his mouth on hers, the soft pressure of it, was almost more than she could bear.

"Neither can you," he said with a little smile. He leaned his forehead against hers. "You can pretend you don't want me, sweetheart, but your kisses speak the truth."

"The truth," she said coolly, "is that I'm as human as the next woman. You're a charming man, Lord Rashid."

Nick grinned as he took the pilot's seat. "A compliment! Who'd have believed it?"

"Charming, and good-looking, but—"

"Very good-looking. That's what women always tell me."

"And clever," Amanda said crisply. "But I'm not going to be taken in again."

"Do you think I flew all the way to Paris to charm you, sweetheart?"

She looked away from him, folded her arms and stared straight out the windshield. "I don't know why you came, and I don't care. I am not going anywhere with you."

"You *do* care, and you are going with me."

"You're wrong, Lord Rashid."

"I came because I love you, and you love me. And we're never going to be separated again."

"You found me enjoyable." Her voice wobbled a little and she silently cursed herself for even that tiny show of weakness. "Enjoyable, Your Highness. That was your very own word."

Nick sighed. "A bad choice, I admit." He smiled. "True, though. You were wonderful in bed."

Color scalded her cheeks. "Which is why you regret getting rid of me before finding a replacement."

"Amanda. I know I hurt you, sweetheart, but if you'd listen—"

"To what? More lies? More whispers about—about wanting me forever?" Tears rose in her eyes. Angrily, she dashed them away with the back of her hand. "Look, it's over. I slept with you and I don't really have any regrets. It was—it was fun. But now it's time to go back to New York and pick up my life."

"Deanna wrote that article."

"Am I supposed to go saucer-eyed with shock?"

"Hell." Nick sat back and rubbed at the furrow that had appeared between his eyebrows. "Amanda, please. Just give me a chance to explain."

"The same chance you gave me?"

"All right." He swung toward her, eyes glittering, and grabbed her hands. "I was a fool, but now I'm trying to make it right. I'm telling you, Deanna wrote that thing—with Abdul's help."

"Frankly, Lord Rashid, I don't really give a..." Her mouth dropped open. "Abdul? He helped her do such a terrible thing to you?"

"He saw what was happening between us."

"Sex," Amanda said with a toss of her head. "That's what was happening between us."

"He saw," Nick said gently, taking her face in his hands, "that we were falling in love."

"What an ego you have, Your Excellency! I most certainly did not—"

Nick kissed her again. It was a tender kiss, just the whisper of his lips against hers, but it shook her to the depths of her soul. All her defenses crumpled.

"Nick." Her voice trembled. "Nick, I beg you. Don't do this unless you mean it. I couldn't bear it if you—"

"I love you," he said fiercely. "Do you hear me, Amanda? I love you." He lifted her hands to his lips and pressed kisses into each palm. "Abdul listened at the door the night I told you about the double-faced coin."

"He eavesdropped? But why?"

"He must have sensed something even then." Nick stroked a strand of pale blond silk back behind her ear. "The old man knew the truth before I was willing to admit it. I was falling in love with you."

"And he didn't trust me?"

"He wouldn't trust any female unless she was born in Quidar." Nick smiled. "And it would probably help if she had a hairy mole on her chin and weighed only slightly less than a camel."

Amanda laughed, but her laughter faded quickly. "But you believed I'd written that—that piece of filth. How could you have thought that, Nick? If you loved me, if you really loved me—"

"I was wrong, sweetheart. Terribly wrong. And I'll spend the rest of my life making up for it." A muscle flickered in Nick's jaw. "I know it's not an excuse, but—but once I was a man, the only person who loved me for myself was my father. People see me as a—a thing. A commodity. They want what they can get from associating with me. But not you. You wanted what was in here," he said softly, and placed her hand over his heart. You looked beyond all the titles and saw a man, one who loved you. It's just that I was too stupid to trust my own heart.''

"Not stupid,'' Amanda said, and slipped her arms around his neck. "You were afraid, Nick. And I was, too. That's why it took me so long to admit I loved you." She laughed. "Well, maybe not so long. We've known each other, what, four days?''

"We've known each other since the beginning of time,'' Nick whispered, and kissed her again.

"I love you,'' she sighed. "I'll always love you.''

"You're damned right you will,'' he said gruffly. "A man expects his wife to love him forever.''

Amanda's eyes glittered. "Yes, my lord,'' she said, and smiled.

"I have so much to tell you, sweetheart. Things are changing in Quidar. I may not be the Lion of the Desert for much longer.''

Her smile softened. She framed his face in her hands and drew his mouth to hers. "You'll always be the Lion of the Desert to me.''

Sheikh Nicholas al Rashid, Lion of the Desert, Lord of the Realm and Sublime Heir to the Imperial Throne of Quidar put his arms around the woman who'd stolen his heart and knew that he had finally found what he'd been searching for all of his life.

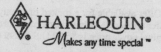

You're not going to believe this offer!

In October and November 2000, buy any two Harlequin or Silhouette books and save $10.00 off future purchases, or buy any three and save $20.00 off future purchases!

Just fill out this form and attach 2 proofs of purchase (cash register receipts) from October and November 2000 books and Harlequin will send you a coupon booklet worth a total savings of $10.00 off future purchases of Harlequin and Silhouette books in 2001. Send us 3 proofs of purchase and we will send you a coupon booklet worth a total savings of $20.00 off future purchases.

Saving money has never been this easy.

I accept your offer! Please send me a coupon booklet:

Name: _____

Address: _____ City: _____

State/Prov.: _____ Zip/Postal Code: _____

Optional Survey!

In a typical month, how many Harlequin or Silhouette books would you buy <u>new</u> at retail stores?

☐ Less than 1 ☐ 1 ☐ 2 ☐ 3 to 4 ☐ 5+

Which of the following statements best describes how you <u>buy</u> Harlequin or Silhouette books? Choose one answer only that <u>best</u> describes you.

☐ I am a regular buyer and reader
☐ I am a regular reader but buy only occasionally
☐ I only buy and read for specific times of the year, e.g. vacations
☐ I subscribe through Reader Service but also buy at retail stores
☐ I mainly borrow and buy only occasionally
☐ I am an occasional buyer and reader

Which of the following statements best describes how you <u>choose</u> the Harlequin and Silhouette series books you buy <u>new</u> at retail stores? By "series," we mean books within a particular line, such as *Harlequin PRESENTS* or *Silhouette SPECIAL EDITION*. Choose one answer only that <u>best</u> describes you.

☐ I only buy books from my favorite series
☐ I generally buy books from my favorite series but also buy books from other series on occasion
☐ I buy some books from my favorite series but also buy from many other series regularly
☐ I buy all types of books depending on my mood and what I find interesting and have no favorite series

Please send this form, along with your cash register receipts as proofs of purchase, to:
In the U.S.: Harlequin Books, P.O. Box 9057, Buffalo, NY 14269
In Canada: Harlequin Books, P.O. Box 622, Fort Erie, Ontario L2A 5X3
(Allow 4-6 weeks for delivery) Offer expires December 31, 2000.

PHQ4002

If you enjoyed what you just read,
then we've got an offer you can't resist!

Take 2 bestselling love stories FREE!

Plus get a FREE surprise gift!

*An electric chemistry with a disturbingly
familiar stranger...
A reawakening of passions long forgotten...
And a compulsive desire to get to know
this stranger all over again!*

Because

**What the memory has lost,
the body never forgets**

In Harlequin Presents®
over the coming months look out for:

BACK IN THE MARRIAGE BED
by Penny Jordan

On sale September, #2129

SECRET SEDUCTION
by Susan Napier

On sale October, #2135

THE SICILIAN'S MISTRESS
by Lynne Graham

On sale November, #2139

Available wherever Harlequin books are sold.

HARLEQUIN®
Makes any time special ™

**Season's Greetings
From**

HARLEQUIN® *Presents*

Give yourself a gift this year!

We've two holiday stories,
written especially for you
by your favorite authors:

THE SICILIAN'S MISTRESS

By
Lynne Graham

#2139

A YULETIDE SEDUCTION

By
Carole Mortimer

#2141

On sale November

Available wherever Harlequin books are sold.

HARLEQUIN®
® *Makes any time special* ™

Visit us at www.eHarlequin.com   HPCHRIS